RICHARD

THE DEATH OF ABBÉ DIDIER

Complete and Unabridged

LINFORD
Leicester

First Linford Mystery Edition
published June 1988
by arrangement with
Victor Gollancz Ltd.,
London

British Library CIP Data

Grayson, Richard
    The death of Abbé Didier.—Large print ed.—
Linford mystery library
    Rn: Richard Corindal   I. Title
    823′.914[F]

    ISBN 0-7089-6562-8

Published by
F. A. Thorpe (Publishing) Ltd.
Anstey, Leicestershire
Set by Rowland Phototypesetting Ltd.
Bury St. Edmunds, Suffolk
Printed and bound in Great Britain by
T. J. Press (Padstow) Ltd., Padstow, Cornwall

For my daughters, Izabel and Madalena

1

THE ball to celebrate the eighteenth birthday of Marie-Thérèse de Saules, although it fell in July, was the most spectacular event of the summer season for Paris society. The "Grande Saison" was almost over and in most years by that time many of the "gratin" or upper crust would have shut up their Paris homes and moved with their wives and children to family châteaux or to a watering place in the Alps or to a fashionable resort like Deauville or Cabourg. This year, however, few had departed for few were willing to miss the grand fête which the banker, Monsieur Armand de Saules, was staging for his only daughter.

As a setting he had chosen the exclusive Tir aux Pigeons in the Bois de Boulogne. On the lawns of the club a vast marquee had been erected and decorated in a style and with a luxury which few Paris drawing-rooms could match. For entertainment the entire corps de ballet of the Opéra, accompanied by an orchestra of 140 musicians, would dance on a stage that had been specially constructed in the lake. For those of the 2,300 guests who might wish to stroll or gossip or flirt in the night air, more than 80,000 Venetian lanterns had been hung in the trees and 15 kilometres of carpet laid to protect their feet from the dew on the grass. The jets of water from the fountains in the lake had been replaced by hissing flames and as a climax to the evening there would be an extravagant display of fireworks.

Gautier moved among the groups of people who were standing near the lake, aware that although like every other man there he wore full evening dress, he was not one of them. The knowledge did not disturb him. At times he wondered whether this was one of the character-istics of a successful policeman, an inner detach-ment which kept him always apart, allowing him to mix with others and at the same time watch and observe. At other times he recog-nized that many of his colleagues in the Sûreté formed close friendships, raised contented families, were accepted in the streets or quar-tiers where they lived. Perhaps it was only he who stood apart, whose wife had left him for another man, who had never even remained with one mistress for any length of time.

He was at Marie-Thérèse's birthday party not as a guest but on duty. The Director of the Sûreté, Courtrand, who had many friends among the wealthy and influential, had suggested to Monsieur de Saules in a friendly way that it might be prudent to have one of his senior inspectors and a few men at the Tir aux Pigeons that evening. It was true, of course, that the wave of anarchism when bombs were being placed in the homes of judges and politicians—even a President of the Republic had been assassinated—had long since subsided. Even so society in Paris had been badly frightened and the fear still lingered. With more than 2,000 people present at the ball including many men of good standing in the administration, one should not rule out the possibility that some malcontent might be tempted to try a spectacular coup. So Monsieur de Saules had accepted Courtrand's advice and Gautier, his principal assistant, Surat, and twenty picked men had been sent to the Tir aux Pigeons; Gautier and Surat in evening dress to mix with the guests, the policemen dressed in silver and blue livery reinforcing the corps of 170 servants who were staffing the party.

Around him Gautier heard laughter and

3

animated conversation. Mostly it was gossip, some of it witty, much of it malicious, the idle malice of a long season that was ending in ennui and irritation.

As he was passing a group of women he heard one of them say: "Have you heard? The Princesse Balakoff has found a new lover."

"I don't believe it!" another woman exclaimed.

The Princesse Balakoff, a young and beautiful Russian, had been the centre of a scandal that had shaken Paris not many months previously. One afternoon her elderly, very rich and very jealous French husband, armed with a pistol, had burst into the bedroom of a discreet hotel de rendezvous where she was entertaining a young and virile lover. He had fired and missed, at which the lover, trying to escape another shot and forgetting perhaps that they were on the third floor of the hotel and not in his ground floor garçonnière, had jumped out of the window naked and fallen to his death.

"She has courage, that one," a third woman in the group remarked. "Who is this new lover?"

"The young Duc de Chinon."

"Then he would be advised to take jumping lessons."

As they stopped speaking, the fountains of fire in the lake were extinguished and the lamps in the marquee lowered, a sign that the ballet was about to perform. Gautier, sensing that he would be conspicuous if he continued strolling among the guests, took up a position by a tree. He was not expecting trouble that evening. The grounds had been carefully searched for hidden bombs before the guests arrived and at the entrance to the Tir aux Pigeons, invitation cards were being thoroughly scrutinized.

From the back of the dimly lit auditorium in the lake, a single ballerina appeared, circling the stage in a series of fouettés and then moving into the centre. Gradually the lights grew brighter and the music louder as the corps de ballet appeared on either side of the stage, forming a semi-circle around the principal ballerina as she continued her dance, pirouetting now and ending in an arabesque penchée.

As he watched, Gautier was aware of a sense of disappointment. Although ballet in France was little more than an appendage to opera, a diversion staged between acts of Gounod and Wagner, whose work following a hostile reception by the chauvinistic French after the disastrous war had now been accepted, the dancers of the corps de ballet were among the most sought-after women in Paris. For many of the dancers their art was no more than a shop-window, an opportunity to display their charms to those who could afford them. During intervals in the performances, subscribers to the Opéra were admitted to the Foyer de Danse, men only of course, where they could meet and talk with the dancers, girls like Julia Subra whom the King of Serbia could not resist, Mathilde Salle, the mistress of the financier Isaac de Camondo, and Mariquita, supposed to be the daughter of an Italian priest and a rich Roman lady, whom Toulouse-Lautrec painted. Even if Gautier had been to the Opéra, he could never have penetrated the Foyer de Danse, the entrée to which was jealously guarded. A man had to be a member of one of the three most exclusive clubs in Paris, the Jockey, the Cercle de la Rue Royale or the Cercle Agricole before he was admitted.

This then was the first time Gautier had seen the dancers perform and he found them, as women, lacking in physical appeal while their dancing, with its formal steps and classic poses, seemed stilted and unnatural. In their white tutus they looked like moths, flitting unceasingly around a bowl of light that was the stage, suspended against the darkness of the lake and against the night sky.

Close behind the tree against which he was leaning, two women were talking in low, serious tones. His attention distracted from the ballet, he could not help but hear what they were saying.

One of the two, who had a deep contralto voice with an attractive huskiness, remarked: "Chérie, you're making a mistake, believe me!"

"Then you consider that I should marry him?" The other woman's voice was younger and she seemed to speak with the impatience of youth.

"Why not?"

"Because he's repulsive and almost forty. I've no wish to bind myself to him for life."

"You don't understand, Chérie. By marrying you wouldn't be giving up your freedom but gaining it. In France a woman has no liberty until she is married."

"I don't see it that way. By marrying a girl merely exchanges one tyranny for another. She escapes from a tiresome mother and an inquisitive confessor only to imprison herself with a male autocrat."

Gautier understood the note of rebellion in what the younger woman was saying. Over the last few years girls of good family had begun to challenge the conventions of society by which the colours of their clothes, the books they might read, the houses they might visit and the hours which they must spend each week with their confessors were all laid down by precept. It was not surprising that they should, because the arrival of the twentieth century had brought a new era for women. Twenty years previously secondary education had been introduced for girls and though it had scandalized the bourgeoisie at the time it was the beginning of emancipation. Medicine, law, the civil service, one after another these bastions of male prerogative fell and were opened to women. A society for the Rights of Women was formed and found a platform for its views in several newspapers for women which began to appear at the turn of the century.

"In spite of what you're saying now," the older woman remarked, "you were ready to marry the comte a month ago."

"As you well know, things are different now."

"Chérie, you are chasing an impossible dream."

Gautier looked over his shoulder. The two women were walking away, still engrossed in their argument. In the darkness he could only make out that one of them was tall and dark-skinned, the other petite and very fair. He wondered without real curiosity who they were.

The first of the two ballets that were to be performed that evening was reaching its climax. "Climax" was too strong a word, because the piece was little more than a diversion, a series of dances held together with a flimsy story of the love of a prince for a captive princess.

As Gautier watched it, he felt a hand laid on his arm. Surat, his assistant, had come up to him without speaking, not wishing to draw attention to himself nor to disturb the entertainment of the other guests.

"What is it, Surat?" Gautier asked quickly. "Trouble?"

"Nothing serious, Patron. We've just picked up Emil Sapin."

"Sapin? Here?"

"Yes. As bold as you like, wearing evening dress and carrying an invitation."

Emil Sapin was one of the most colourful and more successful of the many hundreds of petty criminals in Paris. He was known in the underworld as "le lapin", partly for his skill in disappearing into some bolt hole whenever he was in trouble and also on account of the many children he had fathered with a legion of women. Picking pockets, burglary on a modest scale and a little pimping on the side were Sapin's line of business and he had never aspired to anything as grandiose as anarchism, so Gautier was surprised by Surat's news.

"Where have you got him?" he asked.

"A couple of men are keeping him out of the way behind the tent which the caterers are using as a kitchen."

"You searched him, I suppose?"

"Yes, and we found this."

Surat held out a diamond and sapphire necklace. Even in the darkness it looked expensive, one of those creations fashioned by a jeweller in Rue de la Paix for a man who was devoted to his wife or needed to impress a mistress.

"Does anyone know about this?" Gautier asked Surat.

"No. One of our men spotted Sapin among the guests and we picked him up without any fuss."

"Splendid! Then let's go and see what the fellow has to say for himself."

They found Sapin behind the kitchen tent with two burly policemen. Gautier scarcely recognized the man who, doubtless not wishing to spoil the unaccustomed air of elegance which a tail coat, gleaming white shirtfront and white tie gave him, had acquired and fitted a neat black wig to conceal his total baldness. Before starting to question him Gautier sent Surat to fetch the host of the ball, Monsieur de Saules.

Then he said: "Where did you get it, Sapin?"

"The necklace? I found it lying in the grass, Monsieur l'Inspecteur. The lady must have dropped it."

"Not the necklace. We'll know soon enough from whose neck you stole that. Where did you get that invitation?"

"They are being sold by the score around Pigalle at five sous a time."

"Let me see it."

Sapin handed him a large gilt-edged card elaborately and beautifully engraved. It requested the pleasure of the company of

Monsieur Henri de Brissaude at the grand fête to celebrate the birthday of Mlle Marie-Thérèse de Saules. Gautier examined the card.

"This is one of the original invitations," he told Sapin, "not a cheap printed forgery."

"I wouldn't know about that."

"Where did you get it?"

"If you must know, a friend gave it to me." Sapin seemed unconcerned at being found out in one lie. "I thought I'd come along to see the fun."

"And where did your friend procure the card?"

"A man he knows burgled a house in Neuilly a couple of nights ago. He saw the invitation lying on a table and took it, more for a joke than anything."

"In that case, why has Monsieur de Brissaude not reported the theft?"

"He has left Paris for the summer and locked up his house. That's why my friend burgled it."

There was little doubt in Gautier's mind that the man was lying. Lies flowed from his lips as effortlessly as platitudes from a politician. He would have questioned him some more, but at that moment Surat returned followed by Monsieur de Saules. The banker was a short, slight man with a neatly trimmed beard, a carefully waxed moustache and well manicured hands which moved around a great deal, jerkily and restlessly, like sparrows on a roof. He was the third generation of a family of bankers, whose firm had been one of those who had raised the 5,000 million francs demanded by Germany after her victory in 1870 and enabled France to pay off the indemnity before time and rid herself of the hated occupying troops. France rewards those who serve her generously and not only had the father of Monsieur de Saules been made a Commander of the Légion d'Honneur, but his firm had prospered. Now Monsieur de Saules had a flourishing bank, a house in Faubourg St. Germain, a beautiful and talented wife and all the other possessions which most men covet but few achieve.

Gautier had met the banker in Courtrand's office at the Sûreté a few days previously and found him courteous and kind and evidently, apart from the extravagance of his daughter's birthday party, not a man who splashed his wealth around. As a banker, no doubt, he respected money and when he spent it would expect a better return than just the admiration of his friends or the envy of his enemies. Now, in a few words, Gautier told him how Sapin had been detected and arrested.

"The scoundrel!" de Saules exclaimed. "And has he stolen anything, do you know?"

"Only this necklace, Monsieur." The banker took the necklace and as he was examining it, Gautier added: "Now all we need is to establish who the owner is, return it to her quietly and that can be the end of the matter."

"You have done well, Inspector," de Saules said and then he smiled as though enjoying a private joke as he added: "As for the necklace, I recognize it. It belongs to the Duchesse de Paiva."

Like most people in Paris, Gautier knew the Duchesse de Paiva only by reputation. A former circus rider who had also appeared at the Moulin Rouge, Jeanne Baroche had married a Portuguese nobleman a few years previously and had been admitted reluctantly to Paris society. Not long afterwards the duc had inadvertently been killed in a duel, defending his wife's honour—inadvertently because duels were not supposed to end in anything more serious than a scratch—and his adversary, whose pistol had discharged itself prematurely, had been forced to leave France. The widowed duchesse had been left with a fine house in Avenue des Champs Elysées and much of her youth remaining, but surprisingly she had ceased to scandalize Paris with her exploits and amours and lived quietly and, as far as anyone could tell, alone.

"Take him to the wagon," Gautier told the two policemen who were holding Sapin and the thief was led away to a police wagon which had been left standing unobtrusively a short distance from the Tir aux Pigeons in one of the many copses to be found in the Bois de Boulogne.

"Unless I am mistaken," Monsieur de Saules remarked when the policemen had gone, "here is the Duchesse de Paiva herself."

Two women were approaching. The younger of the two went up to Monsieur de Saules and kissed him on the cheek, saying: "I've been looking for you everywhere, Papa. It has been the most wonderful party."

Monsieur de Saules kissed her back, and then held the necklace out to the other woman. "You've been rather careless, Jeanne, my dear."

"My necklace!" The duchesse gasped, putting her hand up to her throat. "Where did you find it?"

15

The Duchesse de Paiva was dark and must have been in her early thirties. Mademoiselle de Saules had a delicate face which looked as though it had been traced by an artist intent on purity of line rather than depth of expression. Gautier would not have recognized her rather commonplace voice, but the distinctive huskiness of the duchesse was unforgettable. They were the two women whose conversation he had overheard as he stood watching the ballet a few minutes earlier.

2

THE twin towers of the church of Sainte Clothilde reached up from the early morning shadows of narrow streets to a blue sky that would later harden into brightness. The streets were empty except for an occasional servant hurrying off on some forgotten errand and silent, for the horses and carriages of the families who lived in the Faubourg would still be in their stables.

As usual Gautier had arrived early that morning at Sûreté headquarters on Quai des Orfèvres. He had been the first inspector to report for duty and so it was he who had gone to the church of Sainte Clothilde in answer to a call from the police of the seventh arrondissement. Inside the church a small group of people were standing in the nave near the chapel of Sainte Clothilde. Almost all of them were women, domestic servants, shopworkers, grandmothers, and many of them were weeping quietly.

A ray of sunlight, slanting into the dusty

gloom of the church through a broken pane in a stained-glass window, fell across the body of a priest which lay stretched out on the floor of the chapel. A policeman stood by the rail which separated the chapel from the main body of the church and another was standing beside a doctor who was examining the body.

Gautier, who before he joined the Sûreté had been attached to the police commissariat of the neighbouring fifteenth arrondissement, knew the two policemen and he knew Doctor Mercier. He also knew the dead man. Abbé Didier, the vicar of Sainte-Clothilde, was a saintly man who, although his church was frequented by the rich and powerful, was a friend of the poor. Gautier had often seen him in his threadbare soutane, hurrying through the streets of the Left Bank to visit the sick or to hear confessions. The abbé, who had an unshakeable belief in repentance, confession and absolution as a surer road to heaven than pious thoughts and good works, had been tireless in hearing confessions, at any time and anywhere, in people's homes, on park benches, in the streets. Now he lay on the floor of his church with his kindly face and pink cheeks frozen for ever in an expression, not of shock or pain, but of mild surprise.

Doctor Mercier finished his examination of the body and stood up. Seeing Gautier he said: "Good morning, Inspector. The abbé's dead, I'm afraid; stabbed through the heart."

"Did you find a weapon?" Gautier asked the policeman beside them.

"No, Inspector."

"Have you any idea what it might have been, Doctor? A knife?"

"A dagger more likely. Something quite thin and very sharp. One of those Italian stilettos, perhaps."

"We found the abbé in there," the policeman said, pointing to the confessional in one corner of the chapel. "It would appear that he was killed as he was hearing a confession."

"Now who would wish to kill a priest?" Gautier said thoughtfully. "And why?"

"Very strange!" Doctor Mercier agreed. "Bizarre!"

He picked up his bag, shook hands with Gautier and left, promising to arrange for the abbé's body to be taken away. Gautier looked around the chapel. To his right was the altar and above it a figure of Sainte Clothilde, while on the wall beyond a mural depicted her healing the sick. On the opposite wall another mural in the same style showed the conversion to Christianity of the saint's husband, Clovis, King of the Franks.

Between the two murals, against the outer wall of the church and facing into the centre of the chapel, was a confessional. The narrow, closed stall in which the priest sat to hear confessions was flanked on each side by semi-circular alcoves where the penitents knelt. They could speak to the priest through lattice screens, beyond each of which was a sliding shutter. This allowed the priest to converse with a penitent on one side but shut off the person kneeling on the other side by sliding forward the shutter. A brown curtain hung down in front of each alcove, so that the penitent could kneel and make his confession with a degree of privacy.

The door to the priest's stall was open and Gautier looked inside. The abbé's purple stole which must have fallen from his body as it was being taken out into the chapel, still lay on the floor. There was a little blood, but not as much as one might have expected. Some of it had splashed on to the screen on the left-hand side of the confessional which was open, while the shutter on the other side was pushed forward. Evidently the abbé had been stabbed through the screen by someone kneeling or crouching in the alcove beyond.

Gautier sat on the priest's stool, leaning forward and to his left as the priest would have done to hear a penitent. In that position his heart was only a few centimetres from the screen. The screen itself was a lattice composed of narrow diagonal strips of wood which left diamond-shaped apertures about two centimetres in width, easily wide enough to allow for the thrust of a thin, pointed blade.

Outside in the chapel the policeman stood waiting and Gautier said to the man: "Tell me what happened."

"All I know is that a woman came to the commissariat and told us the abbé was dead. My colleague and I came to the church and found him lying in the confessional. We pulled him out and sent for the doctor."

"Is the woman still here?"

"Yes. She's with that crowd over there."

"I would like to speak with her."

The policeman fetched the woman who was about sixty, dressed in black and wearing a black shawl over her head and shoulders. Her face was grey and lined, her hands bony and marked by a lifetime of manual toil. Gautier saw a hundred women like her every day in Paris.

She told him her story; how she had come to the church for confession and finding no one waiting in the chapel had gone and knelt in the confessional. In the light of the small lamp burning inside the priest's stall she had seen the abbé's body slumped on the floor.

"Thinking he might have had a seizure," the woman continued, "I opened the door and tried to rouse him. Then I saw the blood. I went round to the priests' house in Rue de Martignac but there was nobody there, so I fetched the police."

With the aid of a few questions, Gautier learned from her that Abbé Didier heard confessions every morning from six-thirty to seven-thirty, so that the poor people of the parish could come on their way to work and receive absolution for their sins of the previous night. Not many people came to confess at that hour, but the abbé was always in the chapel waiting.

"You say there was no one in the chapel when you arrived?" Gautier asked the woman.

"No, Monsieur. Neither in the confessional nor waiting in the chapel."

"You saw nobody in the church at all?"

"A woman was leaving the church as I arrived."

"Did you recognize her?"

"No, she was some distance away but in any case she would not be anyone I know."

"How can you be sure?"

"She was a lady. You could tell by her clothes."

"Did you get the impression that she was an old woman?"

"That's hard to say. On the one hand she was very hunched, bent like an old woman, but she walked without a stick and quite quickly."

"So she was probably middle-aged?"

"Most likely."

While they had been talking a priest, whom Gautier assumed must be one of the two curates attached to the church of Sainte Clothilde, came into the chapel. He looked at the abbé's body, crossed himself and knelt down beside it, his lips moving as he prayed. When he had finished, he went to the altar of the chapel, knelt there and prayed again. Finally he came over to Gautier and introduced himself as Father Xavier.

"I shall never forgive myself, Inspector," he said, "for not being on hand when the abbé needed me."

"Why do you reproach yourself?"

"When they came to fetch me to the church, I was out. Otherwise at least I would have been able to give him the last sacraments."

"I doubt it, Father. He was stabbed through the heart and must have died at once."

"But who on earth would have wished to kill him?"

"I was hoping you might have been able to tell me that," Gautier said.

The curate shook his head. Although he was a tall, spidery man, he had the long mournful face and drooping jaws of an overfed dog. "The poor abbé! If only he had devoted himself entirely to ordinary people, to the people who need our help and spiritual guidance and shunned the idle rich."

There was reproach in his tone. The church of Sainte Clothilde was in the Faubourg St. Germain, that quadrilateral of Paris bordered by the Seine to the north, by Rue de Babylone to the south, by Esplanade des Invalides to the west and by Rue des Saints Pères to the east. Although in recent years some bold families had migrated across the river to the Plaine Monceau or to large new houses along Avenue du Bois, the Faubourg St. Germain remained the home of "le Monde", of the old aristocratic families, of the rich and the well-connected.

Gautier knew that the Abbé Didier had been popular among the wealthy families of the district, if not for his saintliness, then for his scholarship, his culture and his wit. He was confessor to their daughters and very often a guest at their dinner tables, where he would listen to the conversation and argue good-naturedly on manners and morals with philosophers, scientists and writers.

"When I tried to advise him," Father Xavier added, "he told me that no one was worthless."

"Do you know if he had any enemies?"

"Who knows? He never did an unkind or a malicious act in his life, but then even good deeds can cause anger or resentment; too often there is someone who believes himself wronged."

"Did he seem troubled or in any way concerned this morning?"

"Alas, I did not see him this morning, Inspector. He made it a rule to rise early and come to the church to hear confessions and he would stay here throughout even if nobody came. He would say that sitting waiting in the confessional at least gave him time to reflect on his own failings and sins."

"Then when did you speak with him last, Father?"

"It must have been at lunch yesterday." Again there was disapproval in the curate's tone as he continued: "The abbé dined with one of our wealthy parishioners last night. He was confessor to their daughter and they were celebrating her eighteenth birthday."

Gautier's interest quickened. "Would that have been the daughter of Monsieur de Saules?"

"Yes."

"Then the abbé was at her ball in the Bois de Boulogne?"

"Heavens, no!" Father Xavier was shocked. "He would never have attended such a frivolous affair. But before the ball, the family had a small, private dinner for intimate friends."

3

RUE DU BAC was one of the narrow streets of old Paris that had escaped unscathed when Haussmann had demolished large areas of the city some forty years previously to build the great boulevards and tree-lined avenues that foreigners so much admired. Running southwards from the Seine, it was flanked by several fine old "hôtels particuliers" which had been the homes of aristocratic families for generations. One of them, formerly owned by a minor branch of the French royal family that had been totally erased by the revolution, had been bought, beautifully restored and discreetly modernized by Monsieur Armand de Saules.

The large, green wooden doors of the archway which led from the street to the property stood open and beyond them Gautier found himself in a paved courtyard with the house on one side and stables on the other. Outside the stables stood an elegant landau with its liveried coachman ready on his box, its twin grey horses patiently waiting.

A manservant opened the door of the house and when Gautier said that he wished to see Monsieur de Saules, he was told that the master had already left home for his office. Few businessmen in Paris would have been at work so early but that, Gautier supposed, might have been one of the reasons for the banker's success. He asked if he might see Madame de Saules instead and was taken to wait in a room on the first floor of the house, while the manservant went to find out whether his mistress would receive the visitor.

Madame Renée de Saules was a celebrity. A Belgian by birth, she had lived all her life in France and by the time she was sixteen was known throughout Paris for her precocious learning and her brilliant conversation. A volume of poems which she published when not yet eighteen had been received by even the most censorious critics with euphoric praise. After she had married Armand de Saules more books of verse followed and in a few years she was accepted as one of the greatest poets in France and even in Europe. At the height of her fame her name had been linked with that of Paul

Monceau, one of the most gifted and most handsome writers of the day. People said it was a marriage of brilliant minds which developed inevitably into a more physical attachment. The affair provided material for newspaper gossip for three years or more, especially since neither her husband nor Monceau's wife appeared unduly concerned at the relationship.

Then suddenly Renée de Saules had stopped writing, had almost disappeared from the literary scene and had apparently retired from society. For several years no poems of hers had been published either in any of the literary reviews or in book form. No one knew why. Some said she had become a recluse, seldom leaving her home and receiving only her most intimate friends. She was supposed to spend whole days in bed with only a bottle of mineral water and a book to sustain her. It had only been at the beginning of the present year that her long silence had been broken and Grasset had published another volume of her poems. Even so she still led a retiring life, appearing at social functions very infrequently and never entertaining in her own home.

For this reason Gautier believed it was unlikely that she would agree to see him that morning and he was surprised when the manservant returned to say that Madame de Saules would receive the inspector if he would be kind enough to wait for fifteen minutes. As he waited, Gautier looked round the room which evidently served as both a lady's drawing-room and a study. On a carved oak writing-table stood a photograph of Madame de Saules by Nadar, while two portraits in oils by Boldini, one of the poetess and one of her daughter as a little girl, hung on the panelled walls.

In a bookshelf along one wall were the works of great French writers, La Rochefoucauld, Voltaire, Chateaubriand and the romantic poets Lamartine, de Musset and de Vigny. The works of Renée de Saules herself, beautifully bound in light blue leather, had a place of honour on one shelf, flanked by the books of her contemporaries, Maurice Barrès, Mallarmé and Lucie Delarue Mardrus.

The most recent book by Renée de Saules, a collection of poems published under the title of *The Unforgiving Life*, lay on the writing desk. Picking it up, Gautier flicked through the pages. He knew little of poetry beyond what he had been taught at school but he had heard literary friends speak of Renée de Saules as a romantic poet whose great forte was lyrical descriptions of love and of pastoral scenes. So, glancing through the book, he was surprised at the pessimism of many of the poems and their frequent references to death and eternity. He began to read and became so engrossed that he did not hear the door behind him being opened.

"Good morning, Inspector Gautier. What are you doing here, may I ask?"

He turned round and saw that it was Marie-Thérèse de Saules who had spoken. "I'm waiting to see your mother," he told her.

"You're not going to discuss the matter of Jeanne's necklace with her, I hope." Marie-Thérèse smiled but the implication of her remark escaped Gautier. "That would be very tactless."

"No. Regrettably I have distressing news for her. Abbé Didier is dead."

"Dead? How?"

"He was mortally stabbed in his church this morning."

Marie-Thérèse frowned thoughtfully without making any comment. She did not seem as surprised by the news as she had been to find Gautier in her mother's apartments.

"I understand the abbé was a frequent visitor to your home, Mademoiselle."

"Yes. Some people might have thought too frequent."

"Are you saying he was not always welcome here?"

"Let me put it this way. My mother saw him constantly. He was her confessor and her confidant. Unfortunately she assumed that others would wish to have the same relationship with the abbé."

"But you did not share that view?"

"No," she said shortly and then added indignantly: "The abbé was my confessor but I believe that priests should give advice only on spiritual matters. They have no right to interfere in a girl's life and in her decisions."

The knowledge that the abbé was dead seemed not to soften the irritation which he had caused her while he was alive. She evidently felt no pity nor sympathy for him. Gautier would have liked to have pressed the conversation further and to ask her more about her relationship with the dead priest, but he decided that she would see this too as an interference in her private life. So he said nothing.

"My mother will be very distressed by what

you have told me," Marie-Thérèse said, abruptly, as though she sensed that he thought her unfeeling. "Perhaps it would be best if I broke the news to her, Inspector."

"Whatever you say, Mademoiselle."

She turned to leave the room but as she did so, the manservant came in followed by another visitor. It was a man in his late thirties, tall, slim and elegantly dressed almost to the point of effeminacy. He carried a top hat and a fine, silver-topped walking stick.

"The Comte de Menilmont is here to see the mistress," the manservant announced and then added, perhaps as a rebuke to police inspectors who arrived uninvited at the house: "By appointment."

When the Comte de Menilmont saw Marie-Thérèse, he drew himself erect and gave a slight, stiff bow. "Mademoiselle, good morning."

Marie-Thérèse looked at him coldly and returned his greeting: "Good morning, Monsieur." Then she left the room.

Since Gautier had been concerned not long previously in two cases in which the wealthy bourgeoisie and minor aristocracy had been involved, he had begun reading the society pages of the newspapers. He had seen the name of Comte Raymond de Menilmont at or near the top of many lists of guests attending the dinner parties or receptions in the salons of fashionable hostesses. The comte, he had understood, was himself a poet, an aesthete and an arbiter of tastes and trends in the literary and artistic world of Paris.

This morning his frigid reception by Marie-Thérèse de Saules appeared to have incensed the comte. Ignoring Gautier he strode to one of the windows of the room and stood looking out, his arms folded and his mouth set in a tight line of displeasure.

"I fear, Monsieur le Comte, that the news I brought this morning has upset Mademoiselle de Saules," Gautier said, without knowing why he was making excuses for the girl.

"Before deciding whether I wish to have conversation with you, Monsieur," the comte replied stiffly, "I would like to know who you are."

"Inspector Gautier of the Sûreté."

"I see." De Menilmont considered this piece of information as a fastidious eater might look at a tarnished fork. Then he asked with some reluctance: "And what is this news of which you speak?"

"The Abbé François Didier has been assassinated."

"Do you mean the vicar of Sainte-Clothilde?"

"Yes." Briefly Gautier explained how the priest had been stabbed to death in his church that morning.

"You probably expect that I should be surprised," the comte said when he had finished, "but I have to say I am not."

"May I ask why not?"

"Because in France today and particularly in Paris, priests have been allowed to usurp a role for which they are not qualified and for which they were not intended. This has happened because the bourgeoisie do not understand how to treat priests in much the same way as a parvenu does not understand how to treat servants. The aristocracy, on the other hand, has never had any difficulties with the church. For more than five hundred years my ancestors had the gift of two livings to bestow on their estates. They used the power wisely and they chose their priests well. It is God who should be worshipped, not priests."

"Some people might say that the priest represents the voice of God."

"Then they would be wrong. Priests are a means of communicating with God, nothing more. They are to be used at the right times and in the right way; for baptisms, for marriages and to give the sacraments."

"Are you saying you believe they have been given too much power?"

"By the bourgeoisie, yes. The church has been invested with power and then when the priests try to use it, the self-professed champions of liberty—the second-rate poets, the journalists and the minor civil servants— protest. That is the root cause of anti-clericalism in France today."

"Do you think it was one of these anarchists or atheists who killed the abbé?"

"Of course. Who else would?"

Gautier had no answer to his question, although he did not believe that the killing of Abbé Didier was in any way connected with the current of anti-clerical feeling which had existed in French politics for some years. If those who opposed the church had wished to make a symbolic sacrifice, they would have chosen someone more powerful and more political than

36

the Abbé Didier; a bishop or even a cardinal. In any event, he was saved from having to reply to the comte's question for at that moment Marie-Thérèse returned to the room.

She walked straight up to the Comte de Menilmont. "Monsieur, I regret that my mother is completely shattered by the news which the inspector has brought us. At present she feels she could not bear to see anyone, not even an old friend. She asked whether you would be willing to return later; perhaps this afternoon?"

"Of course, Mademoiselle. I fully understand. Please tell your mother that I am always at her disposal."

The comte bowed slightly and then left the room. There was a stiffness and self-restraint in his bearing that reminded Gautier of army officers he had met, although as far as he knew, the comte had never served in the army except possibly for his period of compulsory military service, and a man with the right contacts and influence could even get exemption from that.

When the two of them were alone, Marie-Thérèse turned towards Gautier. Believing he knew what she was about to ask him, he said: "Naturally, Mademoiselle, your mother will not wish to see me either. Perhaps I too might return on another occasion."

"If you wish, Inspector, certainly. On the other hand perhaps I might be able to assist you."

"In what way?"

"One cannot suppose that you came to our house today merely to tell my parents of the abbé's death."

"What other reason could there be?"

"You must know that the abbé is not only my mother's confidant but a close friend of our family. You may also be aware that he dined in our house only yesterday. I imagine you may be hoping that my mother might be able to throw some light on the matter of his death."

"I cannot deny that I was thinking along those lines."

Marie-Thérèse sat down on one of the two divans in the room, without inviting Gautier to do the same. She was wearing a silk dress with a skirt composed of alternate panels of black and grey. With its long sleeves and high neckline it would be suffocatingly hot later in the afternoon of a July day, but young girls were not expected to wear bright colours and convention, Gautier knew, was more important to women than comfort.

"Don't misunderstand me, Inspector," she said. "I cannot imagine that anyone could ever wish to kill a priest, but it has to be recognized that Abbé Didier, although he was much loved by the poor, had made enemies among the rich."

"In what way?"

"Let me give you an example. A few years ago the abbé was imprudent enough to decide that the church should take a public stance in the Dreyfus affair. He preached sermons criticizing the government's handling of the case and attacking anti-semitic feeling. That was bad enough for a priest whose church is in this quartier, but Abbé Didier went further. My mother, as you know, is a poet. She has never shown any interest in politics. Well, the abbé persuaded her that it was her duty as a Christian to support the Dreyfusards and oppose all those who supported the army and who believed the wretch got no more than he deserved."

"I see."

"At that time my mother's poetry was very much in vogue." Although she did not say so, Marie-Thérèse's tone suggested that she found it difficult to understand why her mother's verses should ever have been so highly regarded. "She was greatly in demand, invited to all the leading salons where people would gather round to hear her recite a poem or simply to listen to her conversation. On the abbé's advice she then decided she would no longer go to the home of any hostess who had declared herself against Dreyfus. One of the women whose salon she deserted in this way was Madame Trocville."

Among the many hostesses in Paris who held regular soirées in their houses, there were perhaps five or six whose names were known even to those who had never been invited to any salon. One was the Comtesse de Greffulhe, another was Madame Aubernon de Nerville and a third was Madame Geneviève Trocville. Leading newspapers published accounts of their soirées at which writers like Anatole France and Maurice Barrès, artists like Rodin and Bonnat, musicians like Caruso and Debussy and theatrical personalities like Bernhardt and Sardou entertained less celebrated and less gifted guests with their clever conversation.

"What was worse," Marie-Thérèse continued, "was that my mother, under the guidance of the abbé, persuaded some of the other well-known writers to desert Madame Trocville. One was a particular friend of my mother, Paul Monceau, who was also the lion of Madame Trocville's drawing-room. Relations between Madame Trocville and my mother have never been the same since that day and I am sure Madame Trocville has never forgiven the abbé for his interference. Certainly he has never been invited to her house since."

"You're not suggesting that this Madame Trocville could be implicated in the abbé's death?"

"Of course not! That would be absurd! As I said that was just an example of the enmity that the abbé sometimes aroused."

Gautier prepared to leave. He was beginning to be irritated by the way she kept him standing while she spoke to him, but in addition to that instinct told him that he would learn nothing of any consequence from her about Abbé Didier's death.

"I'm sorry I cannot be more helpful, Inspector," she said, as though once again she had sensed what he was thinking. "Is there nothing else you wish to ask me?"

"Only one more thing, Mademoiselle. Could

you let me know the names of the people who dined here before your ball last night?"

"Certainly." Her smile was mocking. "My mother's secretary could prepare a list, although of course that would take some time."

"I understood that only intimate family friends were present at the dinner."

"Yes, but we have many friends. I believe that one hundred and eight sat down to dinner."

On his way downstairs Gautier was impressed, as he had been in Madame de Saules' study, by the décor of the house. The furniture was classical, beautiful pieces of the Louis XV and Louis XVI periods, the carpets and curtains luxurious in material and making, but serving as no more than a tasteful background. In their simplicity of style, the furnishings offered a remarkable and, to Gautier at least, a welcome contrast to the fashion of the day. The other houses of wealthy families which he had visited had been decorated with a bewildering assortment of furniture, ornaments and bric-à-brac. This was the popular vogue and hostesses, influenced perhaps by the bold extravagances of art nouveau, filled every room in their houses almost to suffocation with bibelots and mementoes, inlaid boxes, Venetian glass, coins and medallions, peacocks' feathers, miniature busts of famous composers, imitation Egyptian relics, Japanese screens and a profusion of sepia photographs in silver frames. Even the picture postcard, invented by a Marseillais, Dominique Piazza, some fifteen years previously, was considered worthy of a place in drawing-rooms where royalty was entertained.

Gautier wondered whether the restraint and purity of style in the home of Monsieur de Saules was a reflection of his wife's taste and culture or of the mood which had impelled her to turn away from the frivolity of Paris society.

In the courtyard outside the house a familiar figure was waiting. Surat, his principal assistant at the Sûreté, was a man approaching retirement whose ability and loyalty had apparently never been recognized and certainly never been properly rewarded. He was not only conscientious and brave, but shrewd and diplomatic. Gautier was fully aware that the successes he had enjoyed in recent years would not have been possible without the help and support of Surat.

"If you wanted me, why didn't you come into the house?" Gautier asked.

"I did not wish to disturb you. Besides," Surat smiled and shrugged his shoulders. "I never feel comfortable in these museums where the rich live!"

"I suppose you wouldn't be here if you didn't have news for me."

"That's true, Patron."

"Then what is it?"

"A message from the seventh arrondissement. They are bringing in Abbé Didier's house-keeper to us."

"Oh, yes. Why?"

"Apparently she has admitted to killing the abbé."

4

WHEN he reached the headquarters of
the Sûreté, Gautier was told that the
Director wished to see him as a
matter of urgency. He went straight up to the
Director's office on the first floor and found
Courtrand, who had clearly only just arrived at
Quai des Orfèvres, opening his morning post.

Having always admired the Prince of Wales,
Courtrand had decided, now that Edward was a
monarch, to express his admiration in a slavish
imitation of the Englishman's dress and appearance. For him this was not difficult since,
already small and stocky, he had in recent years
declined into paunchiness and was losing his
hair. He was inordinately proud though of his
greying beard and moustaches and stroked them
frequently with affection.

"Ah, Gautier! Tell me all about it," he said
affably. "How did things pass off?"

The question surprised Gautier. He had
expected that Courtrand would have heard of
Abbé Didier's death and that it was about this

45

he wished to question him with such urgency. "What things, Monsieur le Directeur?"

"The fête of Monsieur de Saules in the Tir aux Pigeons, of course."

"Apart from one small incident which we were able to handle quickly and quietly, there was no trouble." He went on to tell Courtrand how Emil Sapin had been caught with a stolen necklace and how this had been immediately returned to its owner.

"Excellent! And you say Monsieur de Saules was pleased."

"He congratulated me on the way things turned out."

"Excellent!"

Courtrand's appointment as head of the Sûreté had been political, a reward for some service to the government of the day, now no doubt forgotten by all except himself. He repaid this piece of patronage by a tireless concern for the interests of important people, politicians, bankers and aristocrats and a determination that if it were within his power, they would never be embarrassed by any hint of scandal or any suggestion that they might be associated even distantly with anything so vulgar as a crime.

"I've just returned from the home of

Monsieur de Saules, as it happens," Gautier told him.

"What took you there?"

"The Abbé Didier was assassinated in his church this morning."

"Yes, I heard about that," Courtrand said impatiently, "but how does it concern Monsieur de Saules?"

"The abbé was Madame de Saules' confessor and confidant. She supported his church and his many good causes with great generosity. I thought she should know of his death at once."

"Yes, you were right, I suppose."

"Besides, he dined at her house last night," Gautier added. It was a calculated piece of mischief, said tongue-in-cheek, but a reminder to his chief that not everyone believed in the infallibility of the rich. "So she and her dinner guests must have been the last people to see the abbé alive."

"God in Heaven!" Courtrand's reaction was entirely predictable. "You're not starting that nonsense again?"

"Nonsense, Monsieur?"

"Why do you have this obsession," Courtrand went on angrily, "that people of good standing are involved in every crime?"

"Sometimes they are."

Gautier's interruption was ignored. "You cannot possibly believe that any of the friends of Monsieur and Madame de Saules could be implicated in the death of Abbé Didier."

"Probably not. The police of the seventh arrondissement are bringing in the abbé's housekeeper who, it seems, has confessed to killing him."

Only with the greatest difficulty was Courtrand able to retain his self-control. He said stiffly: "In that case, Inspector Gautier, go and take her statement at once."

They brought Madame Bize, the priests' housekeeper, to Gautier's room, a tall, lean woman with the discontented face of one who had spent her life looking after and worrying over other people, not because she cared about them but through a sense of duty. For some ludicrous reason of their own, the police from the Seventh had brought her handcuffed to the Quai des Orfèvres. Gautier told Surat to place a chair so that she would be facing him across the table and had the handcuffs removed.

"Now, Madame," he began, "there are some questions which I must put to you."

"Are you the juge d'instruction?" she asked defiantly.

"No, the inspector in charge of the case."

"I wish to make a statement to the juge d'instruction."

"It remains to be seen whether one will be appointed."

"But one must be!" Madame Bize protested. "I have confessed that I killed the abbé."

"That is so, but we still have to decide whether you are to be believed."

Gautier's comment disconcerted the housekeeper. She had clearly never considered this possibility. "I can tell you exactly how I killed him."

"Before you do that, Madame, tell me why you killed the abbé."

"I had my reasons." She pressed her lips together in a thin line of disapproval.

"We shall need a more convincing explanation than that. You would not have been engaged as housekeeper at the priests' house unless you were a woman of strong Christian convictions and regular religious observance. To risk damnation by killing a priest, you would need a powerful motive."

"The abbé was an immoral man. He deserved to die!"

"What form did his immorality take?"

"Amongst other things, he seduced my daughter."

Gautier almost laughed. The idea that the abbé, elderly, frail and saintly, could possibly have seduced any girl was so preposterous as to be farcical. But the passion in the housekeeper's voice and the light in her eyes were those of a fanatic and he knew from experience that it was dangerous to laugh at fanaticism.

"You must be mistaken, Madame."

"Not at all. My daughter told me as much."

Indignation jerked away all constraint and her story rushed out, almost incoherent in a flood of words. Nicole, her daughter, was a good girl, a girl who had been brought up in innocence, purity and a fear of God, a girl who attended Mass regularly, confessed once a week and went every Tuesday evening to sew garments for the poor with the Little Sisters of Charity, a girl who had a good job at the store A La Samaritaine and gave her wages to her mother. Could the inspector imagine her mother's horror when she learnt that Nicole was to have a baby? Did he realize the shame and disgrace for the family? Nicole had said that one of the priests was responsible and of course it had to be so, for the girl was never alone with any man outside her home. On the other hand the abbé would know the way to her bedroom. It was monstrous.

When her story was finished, Gautier turned to Surat. "Go round to the Samaritaine and bring Madame's daughter here."

"She cannot leave her work!" the house-keeper exclaimed.

"We are on excellent terms with the management of the store. They will not penalize the girl for coming to assist the police." Surat left the room and Gautier continued: "Let us assume, Madame, that your daughter was seduced by one of the priests. Why should you have decided it was the Abbé Didier?"

"For other reasons."

"And they are?"

"He has shown his immorality in other ways. All his life the abbé had led a chaste and holy life. I know that, Monsieur, but he was becoming old. His memory was failing. Age can affect a man in strange ways. Only a week ago I found an immoral book in his bedroom."

"What kind of book?"

"It was a romance called *Mytilène* by Juliette Prévot, a filthy, perverted book!"

Gautier had heard of the novel, for it had created a minor scandal when it had been serialized in *Gil Blas* several weeks previously. Written by a clever young woman journalist, it narrated the story of a girl who, while a novice in a religious order, had been corrupted by a degenerate aristocrat and who had revenged herself on life and on God by corrupting in her turn the mother superior of the order, before abandoning religion to set up a strange ménage with a male homosexual. The daring theme of the book, together with several salacious passages and titillating descriptions, had been attacked by many critics while others had praised its boldness, the originality and freshness of the writing and the brilliant dialogue.

"A revolting book like that!" Madame Bize continued. "They say it is about the fall of a religious into mortal sin. If he would read that, the abbé would be capable of anything!"

"Now that I know your reasons for wishing to kill the abbé," Gautier said, "tell me exactly how you killed him."

"I knew that he heard confessions every morning in the church," she said, confidently, as if she was being interviewed for a position and had been waiting for this opportunity to demonstrate her ability and qualifications. "And I knew that only a few people ever went; sometimes no one at all."

Her story was a long one, carefully told and lovingly embroidered. Gautier listened, in no hurry because he was waiting for her daughter to arrive. A La Samaritaine was only a few minutes' walk from the Sûreté across Pont Neuf and Surat would probably have gone there in a fiacre. Madame Bize told him how she had gone to the church of Sainte Clothilde, found nobody there except the abbé alone in his confessional and stabbed him to death. She spoke of the gloom of the church, the flickering of the candles, the strangled cry from the abbé as he died.

"And what did you do with the weapon?" Gautier asked her when at last she was done.

"The weapon, Monsieur?"

"Yes. What did you use to stab him?"

The housekeeper's hesitation was only momentary. "A knife. One of the knives from my kitchen. It was one of those butcher's knives, very strong, with a broad blade and extremely sharp. After I killed the abbé I took the knife up to the Seine and threw it in the water."

As he listened, Gautier had been scribbling some notes, half-heartedly and more as a matter of form than because he believed they would serve any purpose. Now he put his pencil down as he said quietly: "Madame Bize, why did you invent this story?"

"Are you accusing me of telling falsehoods?" the housekeeper demanded indignantly.

"You did not kill the abbé. We know that. He was not stabbed with a kitchen knife, you see, but with a thin dagger, an old-fashioned weapon in all probability, maybe an antique."

She stared at him, in surprise at first and then with defiance. Then suddenly she collapsed and began weeping, covering her face with her hands to hide the tears.

"Do not distress yourself, Madame," Gautier said, wishing to be kind. "No harm has been done."

"I wish I had killed him," she replied between her sobs and repeated: "He deserved to die."

"As to that, shall we wait and see what your daughter has to say?"

They did not have long to wait. Nicole was

a girl of about eighteen, not particularly pretty but more smartly dressed than most working girls, though the Samaritaine might encourage that, Gautier supposed. She came into the room looking sulky and rebellious, accompanied not only by Surat but by the curate of Sainte Clothilde, Father Xavier. Surat explained that he had found the priest downstairs waiting to see the Inspector and had brought him up.

"Forgive me for intruding," Father Xavier said. His flabby jowls shook with agitation. "But when I heard that Madame Bize had given herself up for killing the abbé, I was distraught! It cannot be true! She is a good woman, Inspector, hard-working, dutiful, religious."

"Do not upset yourself, Father," Gautier replied, smiling. "Madame Bize has now confessed that her confession was mistaken."

"But Mama!" Nicole cried. "Why in heaven did you do such a thing?"

"I should have killed him!" her mother said, mechanically, as though she had convinced herself of this idea without believing it. "Did he not seduce you?"

"Me? The abbé?"

"Madame Bize! Do you know what you are saying?" Father Xavier was shocked.

"You told me it was a priest."

"But not the abbé. Don't be absurd!"

Not until the words were out did Nicole realize the implications of her denial. If her seducer had not been the abbé, he had to have been one of the two curates. She glanced sideways at Father Xavier and her face turned pink. If she can still blush, Gautier thought, then there must be hope for her.

"Come now, Mademoiselle," he said as sternly as he could. "It was not a priest who was responsible for your condition. Admit it!"

The girl looked sullenly first at him, then at Father Xavier and then at her mother. "All right, it wasn't a priest if you must know. Anyway what does it matter?"

"Of course it matters!" Madame Bize shrieked at her. "Who was it then?"

"A boy I met at work."

"God of mercy! But when did you . . . ?" Her mother left the question uncompleted.

"I've been seeing him on Tuesdays, instead of going to the Sisters of Charity," Nicole said coolly and then as though to justify her behaviour she added: "He's given me a good time. We've been to caf'concs, a bal musette, everywhere."

"Mother of God!" the housekeeper wailed. "A bal musette! You've deceived me, you've deceived the church, you've fornicated! You're no better than a whore!"

"Now, Madame Bize," Father Xavier interposed. "Compose yourself, please."

"This will be the end of us. I shall lose my position. Who else will employ me?"

"No more of this scene!" The priest rebuked her firmly. "We must not bother the Inspector with your troubles. The three of us must go home and discuss this calmly and sensibly."

"An excellent suggestion, Father," Gautier said, although privately he doubted whether the church could provide a ready solution to this family problem.

As Father Xavier began to shepherd the weeping housekeeper and her sullen daughter out of the room, Gautier thought of one last question to ask. "Madame Bize believed it was the abbé who had seduced her daughter because he had an immoral book in his possession. Do you know anything of this, Father?"

"An immoral book! That isn't possible."

"She says it was the novel *Mytilène* by Juliette Prévot."

The priest looked at the housekeeper

severely. "This should be a lesson for you, Madame Bize. It is a sin to find sin when none exists. That book did not belong to Abbé Didier; it was lent to him by one of our parishioners who wanted his opinion, the opinion of the Church on it. There is a move to have it proscribed by Rome."

"May I know the name of the parishioner?" Gautier asked.

"I can see no harm in telling you, Inspector. In fact you will find her name and that of the author in a dedication inside the cover. The book was sent to the abbé by Madame de Saules."

5

THE Café Corneille in Boulevard St. Germain had its own coterie of regular customers. There were countless similar cafés in Paris, each of which over the years had come to cater for a particular profession or group of people with common interests. The Café François 1er in Boulevard St. Michel was frequented by Symbolist poets and the Café de La Rochefoucauld in the street of that name was a meeting place of writers and painters, including Degas and Forain and, while he was alive, Toulouse-Lautrec, while in La Rotonde one could find young, avant-garde painters like Modigliani and Apollinaire. There were cafés for actors, for diamond merchants and for bankers. In all of them men gathered to drink a coffee or a bottle of wine or an aperitif, to gossip, exchange news and argue about the issues of the day.

The regular customers of the Café Corneille were mainly lawyers and politicians, which was only to be expected since it was situated not far from the law courts and the Chamber of Deputies. It had also attracted a sprinkling of journalists who preferred it to the Café Tortini where most of their colleagues of the press were to be found. Gautier, who was neither a vain nor a proud man, took a special, private pleasure in knowing that he was accepted by the café's habitués and had many friends among them.

Today when he reached the café soon after noon it was already crowded, but a group of men saw him arrive and beckoned him to their table. One of them was a brilliant and ambitious judge, the youngest judge in France it was said, another an elderly and cynical lawyer, a third a deputy for Val-de-Marne. Seated with them were two journalists, Duthrey of *Figaro*, whom Gautier had known and respected for many years and Vence of *Gil Blas*, a relative newcomer to the Corneille.

"Monsieur Gautier," the judge greeted him, "did I see you last night at the Tir aux Pigeons?"

"Yes. I was at the fête of Monsieur de Saules."

"So? You are rising in the world then?" Duthrey teased him.

"I was on duty. The Director of the Sûreté was afraid lest some agitator might use the occasion for a violent demonstration."

"And did anyone?"

"No. The evening passed off remarkably peacefully."

"Were there no fireworks?" Duthrey asked.

"Yes. At the end of the evening; a fine display."

"I thought there might have been some sparks from the noble Comte de Menilmont," Duthrey said innocently and Gautier realized that he was being mocked, though not unkindly.

"Was the comte there?" the deputy asked.

"I believe so."

"That would be his style; to put on a brave face."

"On the occasions when I've met that young man," the elderly lawyer remarked, "he has never stopped talking about his ancestors."

"Am I missing something?" Gautier enquired. "Why should the comte be upset?"

"It was last night, on her eighteenth birthday, that the betrothal of Marie-Thérèse de Saules to the comte was supposed to be announced. Apparently, however, the young lady changed her mind at the last minute."

"Does anyone know why?"

"Only the family and they have said nothing."

"Everyone in Paris has his own idea of the reason and every newspaper will give a different one."

"I wonder how many of us poor scribblers," Vence remarked, "will have to meet the comte at Longchamps in the early morning."

The racecourse at Longchamps was then a fashionable place for duels. Although strictly speaking duelling was against the law, it was very much in vogue as a means of settling differences or avenging insults. Since the laws of libel and defamation in France were vague and ill-defined, newspapers felt free to publish personal attacks on public figures and even the most scurrilous rumours if these seemed likely to cause a sensation and so boost sales. As a result every journalist of any influence had fought at least one duel and some had fought several. Many even went to the lengths of becoming members of the Club des Mousquetaires in Boulevard des Italiens, where they could receive instruction in swordsmanship from a maître d'armes and in protocol. Duels were fought in accordance with a strict code of rules, jealously guarded by the club, which could be called upon to arbitrate in matters of honour.

"Yes, you had better blunt your pens and sharpen your rapiers," the lawyer said. "Comte Raymond is an excellent swordsman and likes to remind people of the fact."

"The Princesse de Mesagne believes the engagement has been ended because the comte's past has caught up with him in some ugly scandal, blackmail perhaps," Duthrey told them.

The Princesse de Mesagne was the nom de plume of Madame Estradère, who wrote on society affairs for *Figaro*. Duthrey was alluding to the rumours which the gossips of Paris had been savouring for years, that the Comte de Menilmont was a homosexual. The principal reason for the rumours was that he had not only remained a bachelor, but made a habit of engaging as his secretaries a succession of beautiful young men.

"I for one am glad that the marriage is not to take place," said the deputy from Val-de-Marne. "To have allowed it would have been a disgrace; a debauched and profligate man of almost forty and a beautiful young girl of only eighteen."

"Not many years ago,"—Duthrey could find a reminiscence for every occasion—"when he was an ardent champion of her poetry, I recall people saying that the comte was the lover of Madame de Saules."

"That can't be true!" Gautier protested.

"Be fair!" Vence said mockingly. "Forty isn't old for a man and the poor comte has been doing his best to rejuvenate himself. They say he has taken a course of monkey glands."

His remark was a reference to a story current in Paris at that time about a physician who claimed to have discovered a way of restoring the virility of old people by injecting them with an extract derived from the glands of apes.

"Let's not grow sentimental about this affair," the old lawyer told the others. "Each of the two has something the other wants. The comte needs a fortune to pay for his extravagant tastes while his title would secure acceptance in society for the daughter of a Jew."

"She has no need to go to such lengths," the judge argued. "Paris society is much more liberal than it was and Jews of good family are received everywhere."

"No doubt at this very moment there is a group of people in the Café de Flore who would not agree with you."

The Café de Flore was a rendezvous for politicians, writers and journalists of extreme right-wing views. They had declared themselves patriots, in favour of a strong, conservative France and bitterly hostile to radicals, foreigners and Jews. The group had called themselves L'Action Française and published a brilliantly written but often libellous fortnightly pamphlet of the same name as a platform for their views.

As soon as the name of L'Action Française had been mentioned, the conversation at the Café Corneille that morning drifted, as it often did, into politics. The discussion was neither passionate nor acrimonious, because on the whole the habitués of the café were tolerant men of reasonably liberal outlook. Gautier listened to what was being said and from time to time made his comments, but other thoughts were nagging at his mind. He recalled the conversation between Marie-Thérèse de Saules and the

Duchesse de Paiva which he had overheard at the Tir aux Pigeons and in which Marie-Thérèse had expressed her determination to avoid the marriage which had been arranged for her. He also remembered his meeting with her that morning in her parents' home and her hostility towards Abbé Didier for interfering in her life. Could it be, he wondered, that there was a relationship here which ought to be explored?

Before he had left the Sûreté for the Café Corneille, Gautier had given Surat two assignments. The first was to go to the priests' house in Rue de Martignac and look for the copy of *Mytilène* which the housekeeper had seen in the abbé's bedroom; the second was to discover as much as he could about Juliette Prévot, her upbringing, her family and her present circumstances.

When he arrived back in his office after a quick lunch at another, more modest café, he found that Surat with his customary efficiency had completed both tasks. The copy of *Mytilène* was lying on his table. Opening it he found that there was an inscription on the fly-leaf.

To: Madame Renée de Saules,
     With respectful homage and admiration,
                    Juliette Prévot.

He flicked through a few pages of the novel, half-heartedly, because he realized that he would never find the inclination nor the self-discipline to make himself read it. The book fell open at a place where two folded sheets of notepaper had been inserted between the pages by the last reader. They marked a passage which described the corruption of the mother superior by the novice nun. Gautier could see that it was more than mere pornography. The descriptions of sex, although their implications were beyond doubt, were neither detailed nor explicit and the prose was admirable, with that wonderful expressive simplicity of which French is capable, the images brilliant and evocative. Juliette Prévot, he sensed, must have a remarkable talent.

When he had finished glancing through the novel, he unfolded the sheets of notepaper which had been used as a bookmarker. They contained a note addressed to the abbé and written in a small, neat but over-elaborate hand.

More through curiosity than for any real reason, he read it.

Dear Friend,

I am writing to thank you for giving me your opinion so lucidly and so forcefully on the book. Before I heard it I was in two minds, for although the story is repugnant to me I had no wish to denounce the work of another writer whom some people believe to be exceptionally talented. Your views gave me the strength to do what had to be done. By all means keep the book if you wish to discuss it with the Archbishop.

As to the other matter, have you yet had any news about D.P. from your friends in Italy? His reputation is certainly tarnished but we have no facts. I have heard that apart from anything the Church may have to say, there may even be criminal offences! A. is being very patient but as you know the girl is headstrong and who knows what she might do?

Finally I have been thinking on the other subject we discussed, namely the infidelity in my family. You offered to speak to the lady concerned and I leave it to you to do as you think best. All I would say is that I do not complain, believing this is a cross I must bear, perhaps as a punishment for my own sins in the past.

With all respectful homage,
R. de S.

Lying on the table beside the book was the report which Surat had prepared as a summary of his enquiries. Curious to know more about the authoress of the novel, Gautier began reading it.

Confidential Report   *For: Insp. Gautier* Enquiries about Juliette Prévot were made through a bookseller, one of her fellow journalists and a talkative neighbour. Born Juliette Gérard, she is the only child of an army officer and the family home was in Haute Savoie. She was brought up by her father like a boy, being taught to ride, shoot, fence and swim and becoming expert in these masculine arts. At the age of twenty she was married to a Spaniard, Don Nicolas Gonzales y Ribeiro, but the marriage failed, it is said because of her husband's violent and uncontrollable temper. Within a matter of weeks she left him. Though the generous dowry provided by her father was lost, Madame Gonzales had a modest income of her own and she came to Paris, where she found work in the offices of a woman's magazine.

Within a few years, writing under the name of Juliette Prévot and sometimes simply as Juliette, she made a reputation for herself. She now writes a regular feature for *Le Journal* and contributes articles to several reviews. Madame Prévot, to use her literary name, has a small house in Rue Jacob, where, unusually for a woman living alone, her two servants are both men. She is a member of the Society for the Rights of Women and about a year ago she was fined for breaking the edict of the Prefect of Police which forbids women to wear men's attire in public. She lives well, though not extravagantly, settles her bills promptly and is on good terms with her neighbours.

Gautier had finished reading the report and was locking it and the copy of *Mytilène* in a drawer of his table, when Surat came into the room followed by a caller. It was the curate of Sainte-Clothilde, Father Xavier, and Surat explained that the father had come to the Sûreté asking to see the inspector.

"I believed it was my duty to come," the priest said, "remembering our conversation in the church this morning, when we were wondering who might have wished to kill the abbé."

"Ah! Does that mean you have thought of someone who might?"

"No, Inspector. I still cannot conceive that anyone would want to kill such a kind and devout man."

"Then you have remembered something which might have a bearing on his death?"

"Possibly. I will say no more than that," Father Xavier replied cautiously. "On the other hand, perhaps I am wasting your time. The incident of which I am speaking seemed to be of no particular importance at the time and indeed I ask myself whether it is even worth mentioning."

"Tell it to me, Father, and let me be the judge."

Father Xavier told his story in his own way and in his own time. Gautier found himself wondering whether the curate was equally slow and tortuous in his sermons, but he reasoned that this was unlikely. The wealthy parishioners of his church would expect their religious observances to be conducted briskly and with as little discomfort as possible.

The incident which Father Xavier related had happened a week previously. A man, one of their parishioners he assumed, had come to see the abbé late one morning in the sacristy of the church. Father Xavier had been in the church itself and had been passing the door to the sacristy, when he had heard the man's voice raised in anger.

"You are not dealing with an ignorant peasant now," the man had shouted. "I know the laws of the church. In fact it seems I know my rights better than you know your duties."

The abbé had tried to reason with the man and to quieten him, but he would not listen. If anything the priest's conciliatory attitude had only seemed to make him more violently assertive.

"You need not pry into my life any further," Father Xavier had heard him say angrily. "Now you know everything; that I am an adulterer and a fornicator, even a murderer some would say. I told you all. You did not realize who I was when I came into your confessional this morning, did you, Monsieur l'Abbé? But you listened to what I had to say, to the scandals of my life and then you gave me absolution. So remember this. What you now know about me was told to you under the secrecy of confession and you may repeat it to no one."

At that point the curate, realizing that they were talking of an act of confession, had decided that he should not be listening to what passed between priest and penitent and he had hurried away to another part of the church.

"So you heard no more?" Gautier asked the priest.

"No, Inspector. And I am still uncertain as to whether I should have told you what I overheard. It is at least arguable that what the man was saying was part of his confession."

Gautier had no wish to become involved in a discussion on the niceties of ecclesiastical law, so he merely asked Father Xavier: "Have you no idea of who this man might be?"

Father Xavier looked pained, a man divided between duty to the state and to the church. He said reluctantly: "I did not see him, but Abbé Didier kept an agenda in which he noted his appointments. I found the agenda just now and looked in it. His appointment that morning was with a Signor Daniele Pontana."

"Is he one of your parishioners?"

"Not so far as I know. I have never met the gentleman but they tell me he is an Italian poet."

When she received Gautier at her home in Rue Jacob that afternoon, Juliette Prévot was wearing a pair of dark grey trousers, a man's shirt, a pale blue embroidered waistcoat which she had left unbuttoned, and a pale blue cravat. Apart from her clothes there was nothing masculine in her appearance. Her dark brown hair fell loosely to her shoulders, her face was small and delicate, her hands soft to the touch and carefully manicured.

Her study was unmistakably a working room, neither as tastefully decorated nor as tidy as the study of Madame de Saules. A large number of newspapers, from some of which articles had been cut out, were scattered about together with several reviews; *La Revue Blanche, La Revue des Deux Mondes* and the subversive *La Revue Libertaire*. A stack of books, each with an improvised bookmarker of a strip of paper or a pencil between its pages, stood on the floor.

Two paintings in the modern style, views of Montmartre executed in splashes of bold colour, hung facing each other across the room, while from a silver photograph frame on the writing desk a man in the uniform of a general stared severely into space. Juliette Prévot cleared some papers and other debris from a leather armchair and Gautier accepted her invitation to sit in it.

After thanking her for agreeing to receive him, he said, to explain the purpose of his visit: "I wonder whether you knew the Abbé Didier, Madame?"

"Mademoiselle," she corrected him. "My marriage was annulled. In any case I would prefer it if you were to call me Juliette. I am no lover of formality."

"Thank you."

"I know of the abbé of course, although not in his professional capacity. I am not a very ardent Catholic."

"And had you heard that he had been found stabbed to death in his church this morning?"

"Yes, one of my servants told me. The poor people of the quartier can talk of nothing else."

Gautier had brought with him, wrapped in brown paper, the copy of Juliette's novel which Surat had retrieved from Abbé Didier's room.

He undid the parcel and handed the book to her.

"I see from the inscription in the book that it was a gift from you to Madame de Saules."

As she opened the book to glance at the inscription, Juliette's expression changed. When she spoke her tone was resentful. "Where did you get it?"

"It was found in the room of Abbé Didier."

"I see. Well, I suppose I shouldn't be surprised."

"According to one of his curates, the abbé was asked for his opinion of the book by Madame de Saules. She wished to know how the Church felt about it."

"So it would seem that I have the abbé to thank." The veneer of sarcasm did not conceal her anger.

"For what?"

"My book was generally considered to have an excellent chance of winning the Prix Fémina. People who had canvassed the jury told me there was a comfortable majority in favour of it. No one tried to discover Renée de Saules' views, of course, because we all thought she had retired from public life. She has shown no interest in the prize and although officially she is president of the jury, she had not attended a meeting for years. Then, without warning she reappears, takes charge of the jury and by using her influence makes sure that the prize is awarded to another. I wondered why and now I know."

"You believe she was swayed by the abbé?"

Juliette made a noise of contempt. "For some years she has been afflicted by religious mania. Perhaps she found consolation in the Church after her lover abandoned her."

"Losing the prize must have been a great disappointment to you."

"Come, Inspector," she replied scornfully. "You must have known all this or else you would not be here."

He ignored her challenge. Instead he asked her: "What does the prize amount to?"

"In terms of money not a great deal, but the prestige which it carries helps to sell a book." She was silent for a time, as though she were brooding over the injustice which had deprived her of the prize. "Of course it is insignificant when one compares it with the Goncourt."

"One would expect that. The Prix Goncourt is better known and has been established longer."

"That is not the reason. The Fémina is considered inferior because it is a prize for women." One could sense her anger mounting as she continued: "In fact it was a mistake even to allow my novel to be nominated for the prize. Why were women stupid enough to have created the Fémina? Is it because they accept that they are weaker, less intelligent, less talented than men?"

"One would not have thought they need think that, especially in literature."

In no field were women making more progress at that time towards equality with men than in writing and journalism, where during the last twenty years there had been an explosion of feminine talent. Poets like Anna de Noailles and Lucie Delarue Mardrus were acknowledged to be the equal of their male contemporaries; the novels of writers like Sévérine, Rachilde and Colette sold in enormous quantities and every year new newspapers and reviews written and produced by women came into existence.

"Of course men don't accept that we can compete on equal terms with them," Juliette grumbled. "You will be aware that no woman has yet been admitted to the Académie Goncourt?"

Gautier had no wish to be given a lecture on women's rights and he sensed that he would learn nothing more by pursuing the subject of Juliette's frustrated hopes, so he changed the subject. "Are you by any chance acquainted with the Italian writer, Daniele Pontana?"

"By popular account there is scarcely a woman in Paris who isn't."

"He is popular with the ladies, then?"

"Among ladies in society, yes. They say that any woman in the Faubourg who has not slept with the vain, overdressed little monkey feels she counts for nothing."

"Do I sense that you don't like the man?"

"Like him?" Juliette replied with a little spurt of indignation. "He stands for everything I despise in a man! He was a little provincial nobody who went to Venice and tricked a girl of good family into marrying him so he would find a place in society. Then he abandoned her and his children for a string of mistresses, all of them rich enough to pay his bills."

"I see."

She looked at Gautier searchingly. "Why are you interested in Pontana?"

"Simply because I am told he quarrelled with the abbé recently." Gautier saw no reason for concealing his motives from Juliette.

"Does that mean you no longer suspect me of killing the abbé?"

"I never said I suspected you."

Juliette laughed. Her laugh was attractive, not the restrained and affected laugh which many women whom Gautier knew paraded, much as they would show off a piece of jewellery, but the spontaneous, uninhibited laugh of genuine amusement.

"Why did you come to see me today?" she mocked. "Only because you thought I had reason to wish the abbé harm."

"For a devout and saintly man," Gautier commented, "the abbé seems to have created an astonishing number of enemies. I cannot suspect them all of killing him."

Juliette looked at him thoughtfully. He sensed that she had suddenly thought of a plan which required careful preparation. Finally she asked him: "Would you like to meet Pontana? It can easily be arranged."

"How?"

"He is to be the guest of honour at a literary salon this evening. I shall be going and the hostess has often told me I may take a friend to her soirées whenever I wish. A single woman arriving at her home always makes her feel uncomfortable, I imagine."

"Would a policeman be acceptable?"

"If he came with me, yes." She looked solemn but he realized she was teasing him. "You see I have a reputation for the unconventional. One might say it has come to be expected of me."

"And who is the hostess?"

"Madame Geneviève Trocville."

Gautier recalled what he had heard about Madame Trocville that morning. If what Marie-Thérèse had told him were true, there would be at least three people at the soirée that evening who might conceivably have had a reason for wishing Abbé Didier dead. To him this was not a coincidence. Instinct told him that the abbé had been killed not by an isolated assassin for a single or straightforward motive. For part of his daily life the priest had moved in a society based on closely-woven, even inbred relationships. The cause of his death, Gautier felt certain, would be found in an equally complex pattern involving directly or indirectly many people, their ambitions and their disappointments, their grand passions and petty jealousies, their envy and their greed.

6

MONSIEUR and Madame Trocville lived in Avenue Hoche, on the edge of the Plaine Monceau, a residential district rapidly becoming popular among well-to-do bourgeois families. Their home was the ground floor of a new apartment block, an immeuble de rapport as such buildings were called, and it had a very large drawing-room well suited to the social ambitions of Madame Trocville. Moreover, the drawing-room opened on to a small garden into which guests could escape at her overcrowded soirées for air or to enjoy a private conversation or daring flirtation.

On the way from Rue Jacob to Avenue Hoche in a fiacre, Juliette had explained to Gautier that every hostess ran her salon in her own individual way. At the home of Madame Lydie Aubernon, soirées were preceded by a dinner party for twelve chosen people and at both functions guests were rigorously disciplined. Idle conversations and gossip were forbidden and the plump, energetic hostess would bring to order anyone transgressing this rule by ringing a bell. In Madame Trocville's salon things were much less orderly, not because she was more liberal or tolerant—on the contrary she was rigidly conservative in her views and a monarchist in her politics—but because she was careless and untidy by nature. She might have achieved more of her social ambitions had she pursued them with more method and more perseverance.

When Juliette and Gautier arrived at the apartment about thirty people were gathered in the drawing-room. Evening dress was de rigueur on these occasions, even though it was rumoured that some hostesses were beginning to accept more informal attire, and black tail coats and white shirtfronts offered a flattering contrast to the bright colours of the ladies' dresses.

Gautier was introduced to his hostess. She was a woman of about fifty, tall but round-shouldered, with a mass of untidy hair dyed to the colour of burnished copper. After exchanging a dozen words with Juliette and Gautier, she turned her attention to more new arrivals and they walked away. Juliette saw a couple whom she knew, a young writer named

Philippe Borde who was making a reputation with his superb translations of Persian poems and love stories and his wife, and they went to join them.

"She's not wearing the dress, I see," Madame Borde said almost immediately, nodding in the direction of Madame Trocville.

"What dress?" Juliette asked.

"Haven't you heard?"

"It was yesterday evening at the fête of Monsieur and Madame de Saules," Monsieur Borde added.

"In the Tir aux Pigeons? Monsieur Gautier was there."

"And you didn't know?" Madame Borde was delighted at finding not one but two people who had not heard the story which she would now, unless struck down by an act of God, recount. "Madame Trocville and Jeanne Baroche arrived at the fête wearing identical dresses."

"Do you mean the Duchesse de Paiva?" Gautier asked.

"We can't get used to using her title," Monsieur Borde said. "I knew her in her circus days."

"So you never tire of telling everyone," his wife said sharply. "But you were not one of her intimate friends, I suppose. You would have been too poor."

"How did this coincidence of the dresses come about?" Gautier asked quickly. Quarrels between husband and wife made him feel uncomfortable.

"Jeanne's dress was by Doucet; specially made for the occasion, of course. Well, it seems that the little midinette whom Madame Trocville employs to make all her clothes was until recently working for Doucet. She was discharged by the house and took her revenge by stealing the design for Jeanne's dress."

"What a disaster!" Juliette exclaimed, but her irony was wasted on Madame Borde.

"It was, I can tell you. Jeanne had been dining with the de Saules family, so she was already at the Tir aux Pigeons when Madame Trocville arrived. Can you not imagine their horror when they met each other face to face? Madame Trocville stayed at the party for less than half an hour and then flounced away in a white rage."

"They say she sent her husband round the newspaper offices this morning," Borde said, "trying to persuade them not to print the story."

The press in France at the time, besides being the largest, most diverse and most influential in the world, was also the most corrupt. A man with an actress for a mistress, for example, could with a relatively small payment arrange for articles praising her talent and beauty to be published in leading newspapers. Most daily papers, and there were many of them, devoted columns and even whole pages to news of social events. Any hostess of standing saw to it that her soirées, dances and balls were announced in advance in the press and reported after they had taken place. Even children's parties were considered worthy of a paragraph in the social columns.

"I am surprised that Madame Trocville should have been invited to the ball," Gautier remarked. "They say that she and Madame de Saules are not on the best of terms."

"If one wishes to have more than two thousand guests at a party," Madame Borde replied, "one has to include a few enemies."

"Their quarrel has never been serious enough for a complete break," Juliette said. "They have too many friends in common."

"Yes," Borde agreed. "You will notice that the Comte de Menilmont is here, for example."

He nodded in the direction of the doors which opened on to the garden where the comte was standing, surrounded by a group of elderly ladies. He appeared to be lecturing the ladies and although they were listening to him with affectionate admiration, his face wore an expression of arrogant hauteur. Gautier began to wonder whether the man ever smiled.

"No salon or literary gathering in Paris is complete unless Comte Raymond is present," Juliette said. "At least that's what the comte believes."

"Good heavens, Madame!" Borde was clearly shocked. "Are you saying that you don't approve of the comte?"

"I disapprove of all masculine conceit."

"But he has such exquisite taste; in fine art, music, poetry, decoration, jewellery, everything!"

"Art and literature should reflect the life and vigour of a nation, not the fossilized whims of a precious aesthete."

Monsieur and Madame Borde were plainly disconcerted by Juliette's attack on the Comte de Menilmont and presently, on the pretext that they had seen other friends with whom they must speak, they moved away. Gautier decided that however popular her novels and newspaper articles might be, Juliette's direct and uncompromising attitude towards men must make her many enemies.

"Thank God that dreadful woman has gone," she said when they were alone.

"You dislike Madame Borde?"

"She and women like her betray our sex; pretty, frivolous, they fawn on men or flaunt their bodies at them."

Gautier looked at her. As though to emphasize her disapproval of femininity, she was wearing a dark red dress of simple, almost severe cut. Bright colours were in vogue for evening wear that season and even ladies past middle age were not afraid to be seen in yellow or turquoise or vermilion. In her sombre dress, wearing neither a corsage nor jewellery, with her hair simply taken back and tied behind her neck, Juliette looked solemn and intellectual.

Gautier remembered the words of the novelist Emile Richebourg: "Si tu veux être heureux, n'épouse pas un bas bleu." He wondered whether Juliette's hostility to men and her indifference to her appearance were the reason why at the age of twenty-eight she still lived as a single woman or whether she deliberately cultivated the manner and the appearance to keep men away.

While he was looking at her, a slight stir at one end of the room and a murmur of raised voices were signs that the guest of honour for the evening had arrived. The Italian was talking to Madame Trocville and presently she began taking him on a tour of the room, introducing him to her other guests.

In appearance Daniele Pontana was not at all what his reputation as a ladies' man might have led one to expect. Short in stature and with a sallow complexion, he was not especially handsome and his curly black hair had been covered in brilliantine and carefully arranged across his skull in an only partially successful attempt to conceal approaching baldness. If women found him compellingly attractive, it could only have been for his eyes, which were his best feature, dark and intense. His starched shirtfront was fastened with diamond studs, his cuffs with gold and diamond cufflinks and he was wearing five or six rings, some of them large and ornate and set with precious stones.

Presently Madame Trocville brought him over to Juliette and Gautier. She said:

"Maestro, allow me to present to you one of our most talented young writers."

"Signor Pontana and I have already met," Juliette said as the Italian bent over to kiss her hand.

"Of course! How foolish of me!" Madame Trocville said and then, as though to revenge herself on Juliette for drawing attention to her lapse of memory, she added with a bright, malicious smile: "But what a delightful surprise it is, my dear, to find you escorted this evening by a man."

Pontana turned to Gautier. "Enchanted to meet you, Monsieur." His French was perfect and without any trace of an accent. "And what may I ask, do you write?"

"Very little, apart from reports."

"Reports?"

"I am an inspector with the Sûreté."

Pontana turned to Madame Trocville and smiled delightedly. "You see, Madame! France is the only true democracy in the world. In Venice, my little narrow-minded, provincial Venice, to find an inspector of police in the drawing-room of the most cultured, the most beautiful hostess in the country, such a thing would never be possible."

"Maestro, you make me blush with your flattery!" Madame Trocville looked anything but embarrassed.

"We Italians always speak from the heart."

Madame Trocville tapped him playfully on the arm with her fan. Like most ladies of her age, she always carried a fan at any evening function. Fans were so useful and so versatile. They could be used to hide a demure blush, they could be closed sharply to display annoyance, they could discourage the too bold fingers of an admirer.

She led the lion of the evening away to meet other guests. When they had gone Juliette and Gautier also mingled with other people whom she knew. One was Lorette Mauger, a woman of aristocratic birth whose paintings of flowers had suddenly become fashionable, earning her an income much larger than the pittance she had been left by her husband; Léon Regis, a young organist who had recently been awarded the Prix de Rome and would shortly be leaving to study at the Villa Medici; Jacques Frison, a schoolmaster at the Lycée Condorcet where he taught the children of many wealthy families and a leading Symbolist poet.

They also spoke for a time with the Comte

de Menilmont, who came up to them and said to Gautier: "Inspector, I'm surprised to find you here."

"He came as my guest," Juliette explained.

"I wished to meet Signor Pontana," Gautier added.

"That I well understand," the comte said affably. "He's a remarkable fellow and very talented. I myself am looking forward to a long conversation with him, for we have much in common."

"Your poetry?"

"No, my dear chap." De Menilmont gave a short, falsetto laugh. "I was talking about swordsmanship. They tell me he's one of the finest exponents of the old classic Italian duelling."

"Perhaps then I should challenge him," Juliette said and this time she joined the comte in laughing.

"Have you read his book *Il Secolo*?" de Menilmont asked. "No? Well, you should. It's a tour de force, I can tell you."

"Is that the book that was banned by the Vatican?" Gautier asked.

"Yes, although I can't see why. The Church in Italy is a little hysterical about these things."

The comte was taken away by two of his middle-aged lady admirers. Just at that point the conversation in the room was suddenly silenced by a footman in the doorway who banged a staff loudly on the floor to indicate that the mistress of the house wished to address her guests.

"My friends," Madame Trocville said, "tonight, as all of you know by now, we are privileged to have with us a poet from that great cradle of civilization, our beloved Italy." She pointed at Pontana who was standing beside her. "I refer, of course, to my good friend Signor Daniele Pontana. Signor Pontana is not only gracing my drawing-room with his presence tonight. On my entreaty he is going to do us the great honour of reciting one of his most recent poems. Such is his scholarship that he has written the poem in French and tonight will be the first time that it has been heard in France."

Her announcement received a little flutter of applause, most unusual in a Paris salon where by convention people demonstrated their enthusiasm in more restrained forms. It was not after all a public auditorium. Madame Trocville moved on one side and Pontana stepped forward.

"Mesdames and Messieurs, our gracious hostess has spoken of the privilege I am doing you by being here tonight. She is wrong." Pontana smiled with a practised charm. "It is I who am privileged. France, generous as always, has welcomed an exile to her hospitable shores, but I come as a willing exile, eager to drink deeply of the culture, the learning and the wit which has made your country the indisputable leader of the civilized world. The poem I have written and which your hostess wishes you to hear is a simple expression of the emotions which your beautiful city has aroused in me, a symbolic expression of my gratitude. But although I have had the impertinence to write it in French, the noblest of languages, I am only too conscious that my poor Italian accent cannot do it justice." He smiled again, this time mischievously. "And so I have arranged that the greatest actress in France will read my poem to you."

Turning quickly he left the room. Madame Trocville, who had obviously not known of his intention, was puzzled and some of her guests began murmuring in surprise, but in less than

95

a minute Pontana returned, wearing over his head and shoulders a black shawl, which he had either brought with him or borrowed from one of the ladies present. Striking a melodramatic attitude, he began to recite:

Who has not, wandering in Elysian fields,
Tasted the nectar of a nymph's embrace?

It was a long allegorical poem, full of classical allusions which Gautier found difficult to follow, but for a poem written by a foreigner, its construction, the handling of the metre and the choice of phrase and metaphor were astonishingly skilful. There was also something oddly familiar about Pontana's recitation, the low, vibrant voice and the pointing finger.

A woman standing immediately in front of Gautier suddenly hissed to her companion: "Don't you see? He's taking off Bernhardt!"

Gautier could then see at once the resemblance of the impersonation to France's most celebrated actress, Sarah Bernhardt. Another woman exclaimed: "My God! He even looks like her!"

Several of the guests began to laugh but Pontana silenced them with an upraised hand

and continued reciting. When the poem was ended, he gave an elaborate curtsey in the style of an actress acknowledging applause. Madame Trocville's guests were enraptured, with the sole exception apparently of Juliette.

"There will be nothing else this evening except pretentious conversation and gossip," she told Gautier. "So if you have seen enough of our Italian celebrity, I suggest we leave."

"Of course."

They took leave of their hostess and with the help of one of her servants found a fiacre which had its lamps painted green, showing that it came from the Left Bank. Drivers of fiacres were an independent and often truculent tribe who late at night were disinclined to accept any fare which would take them too far from the quartier in which they lived.

Throughout the leisurely journey to Rue Jacob, Juliette appeared preoccupied and her expression suggested that she was brooding over a memory which still irritated her. Gautier did not speak, because he had decided she was a woman who preferred that her moods should be neither questioned nor disturbed.

After a long silence she said: "I am sorry you

were obliged to endure that loathsome Italian's sneers."

"You were not to blame."

"In a sense I was. He was being offensive to you as a piece of childish spite because I once insulted his vanity."

"In what way?"

"When he first arrived in Paris, friends arranged for him and me to meet. It was one of those ridiculous, romantic ideas; an encounter between two brilliant talents. And like most of these schemes, it misfired."

"You were rude to him?"

"He made me a proposition and I laughed at it."

Gautier thought about asking her what form the proposition had taken, but he changed his mind. Instead he said: "I had to admire the panache with which Pontana combined an insult to me with an extravagant compliment to the hostess."

She fell silent again as the fiacre passed through the moonlit streets and crossed the Seine. Not until it came to a halt outside her house did she speak again.

Then she said abruptly: "I was not entirely honest with you this afternoon."

"In what way?"

"I deliberately gave you the impression I was not aware that Abbé Didier had seen my book."

"But you knew he had?"

"Yes. He came to see me uninvited one afternoon not long ago and talked to me about the book."

"What did he say?"

"The usual platitudes. No, that isn't fair. He talked to me about literature and the arts, reminded me of all the great poets and musicians and painters who had served the church and asked me why I could not do the same. His culture and learning were remarkable."

"And what was the result of your discussions?"

"When he told me he had suggested to the Vatican that my book should be proscribed, I lost my temper and sent him packing."

7

"**S**ENSUAL, serpentine, golden . . . with bold eyes, jet-black hair, a huge provocative mouth and a supple, sinuous body which flows into a hundred seductive poses, which can promise, which can entreat, which can enslave." These were the words that *Figaro* had used more than ten years previously to describe Jeanne Baroche, the vedette of the lady riders at the Hippodrome circus. The journalistic bravura had delighted Paris. The description had been read aloud in a hundred drawing-rooms, had been memorized by old gentlemen whose dreams it excited, had been plagiarized by young gentlemen in their love letters and of course had been extensively quoted in the publicity posters of the Hippodrome.

Gautier could remember reading the passage as a young man. Now, as he offered the Duchesse de Paiva a chair, he found himself measuring her against the old description. The body was no doubt less supple, the eyes less bold, the golden skin a little faded, but the duchesse still retained a striking Latin beauty. Although she was dressed in the manner of a society lady, in a long dress with high waist and bustle and a straw hat decorated with ostrich feathers, he thought he could detect in her deportment and in her manner lingering traces of a cocotte's insolent charm. She carried a parasol and a small green velvet pouch.

She had come to his office soon after nine-thirty that morning, without giving the reason for her visit. In the normal way she would have been taken to the Director, but Courtrand believed in working to a leisurely timetable and was seldom at the Quai des Orfèvres before ten-thirty.

After sitting down the duchesse looked around the room and said: "I didn't realize that our senior police officers had to work in such spartan surroundings."

"Discomfort, like a sentence of death, is supposed to concentrate the mind wonderfully."

"Well, it wouldn't do that for me, I can tell you."

They both laughed. "And how can I be of service to you, Madame?" Gautier asked.

"I came to ask what you have done with that man whom you arrested at the Tir aux Pigeons."

"Emil Sapin? He's in prison and in due course he'll appear in court."

"I would prefer it if he were released."

"Are you suggesting that no action should be taken against him?"

"Yes, Inspector."

Gautier did not attempt to conceal his surprise. "But why not, Madame?"

The duchesse smiled at him engagingly, as though she were about to invite him to join her in an unconventional but harmless conspiracy. "Marie-Thérèse de Saules is a very dear friend of mine, Inspector. As I'm sure you know a girl's eighteenth birthday is one of the memorable occasions of her life. For Marie-Thérèse the ball at the Tir aux Pigeons was a wonderfully happy evening, an evening all Paris is talking about and one which she will always remember. Would you want it to be spoiled for her?"

"Of course not."

"But that is exactly what would happen if this creature Sapin was brought into court. At present no one except Marie-Thérèse, her father, you and I know about the little drama over my necklace."

"And my colleagues in the Sûreté."

"Admittedly, but we can rely on them to be discreet. On the other hand if Sapin appears in court some journalist is certain to be there. You can imagine, Inspector, what a vulgar story the newspapers will make of it. Marie-Thérèse's party was supposed to be the most brilliant event of the social season. Everyone of any distinction was there. How was it then that this thief, this shabby little pickpocket was let loose on the guests? By the time the newspapers have finished it will not be one thief, but six, a dozen. Is that not so?"

"You may be right."

"As the host, Monsieur de Saules will be made to appear at best ridiculous, at the worst dangerously negligent. And Marie-Thérèse, who loves her father, will have to share his humiliation."

Gautier realized that her prediction of what would happen if Sapin were to appear in court was almost certainly correct. He said: "I can understand your wish to spare the family embarrassment, Madame, but to have Sapin released without a trial might present difficulties. He has been in prison for two nights."

"Has he admitted stealing my necklace?"

"No, and he isn't likely to."

"Then what is his story?"

"That he found it lying in the grass."

"We must not rule out the possibility that he is telling the truth." The duchesse opened the velvet pouch she was carrying and from it took out the diamond and sapphire necklace. "When I arrived home from the party the other night I found that the clasp of my necklace was broken. See."

Taking the necklace from her, Gautier held it in his hand. Seeing it in daylight he could appreciate the skill and craftsmanship that had gone into its making. The sapphires had been carefully matched and were set in diamonds to form simple floral patterns that were linked by a gold chain. He looked at the clasp. One of the two gold links of which it was made had been forced open in a way that suggested the two of them had been pulled apart. It was possible that the damage could have been caused by someone snatching the necklace from the neck of the wearer, but quite inconceivable that the wearer would not have felt it happen.

"As I'm sure you understand, Inspector," the duchesse said gently, "if I were required to give evidence in court, I would have to say in all honesty that the necklace might easily have fallen from my throat."

"In that case of course . . ." Gautier said and smiled, "you are right. There would be little point in putting Sapin in court. The final decision is not mine, but I will certainly recommend to my superiors that he should be released."

There could be no doubting the genuineness of the Duchesse de Paiva's pleasure at hearing Gautier's words. She was evidently delighted to know that a seedy and incorrigible little thief was not going to be punished for stealing her necklace.

"You have been very understanding, Monsieur Gautier," she said, putting the necklace back in its pouch and rising from her chair.

"Not at all. Now that you have explained the circumstances, I have no choice but to do as you suggest."

"Many other men would have reproached me for my carelessness and for the trouble I have caused—and they would be right." She smiled. It may only have been his fancy, but for Gautier it was not the smile of a duchess but of a court-esan, a smile which offered nothing so vulgar as an invitation, but which suggested that the two of them had reached an understanding out of which, if he so wished, they could fashion a more intimate relationship. "I would like to show my gratitude," she added.

"That isn't necessary, Madame."

"I know, but I would like to. Do you enjoy the circus?"

He laughed. "Doesn't everybody? But I haven't been to one since I was a boy."

"The circus is the great passion of my life. I still love it; the atmosphere and the excitement. I have a box reserved every Thursday evening at the Circus Alfredi. It would give me great pleasure if you would join me and my friends there tomorrow. Bring your wife."

"My wife and I are no longer together."

Gautier sometimes wondered why to tell people this caused him no awkwardness. It was true that several months had passed since Suzanne had left him and she was living, happily it seemed, with a former policeman who owned a café in Pigalle, but did the fact that he felt no resentment prove either that he was not sorry to be rid of her or that he was incapable of any deep and lasting feelings? And if he followed that line of reasoning he would probably finish up by deciding that this was the real reason why Suzanne had left him.

"In that case come alone," the duchesse said without regret for her faux pas nor curiosity. "We might be able to arrange for you to meet one of the circus riders. Some of them are really very beautiful."

"Yes, I know," Gautier smiled as he took the hand which she held out to him and kissed it. "Thank you, Madame. I will certainly accept your offer if I am not on duty."

Two nights in prison did not appear to have affected Sapin's natural resilience. His manner as he sat facing Gautier was one of complacency tinged with insolence. He was still wearing the evening dress in which he had been arrested and had somehow got hold of a fresh rose which he had pinned to the lapel of his coat.

The rose, Gautier sensed, was a badge of defiance. Sapin could not possibly know, however, that he was soon to be released and he might be persuaded to part with a little information if he were led to believe that this might bring him his liberty. When dealing with dishonest rogues, one must sometimes be prepared to compromise one's own honesty.

"I have had you brought here," he told Sapin, "because I have certain questions to ask you. By answering them willingly and frankly, you could make things easier for yourself."

Sapin laughed cynically. "Oh, yes? How much easier?"

"At the worst it would mean a less severe sentence, I can promise you that."

"And at the best?"

"The lady whose necklace you tried to steal might be persuaded not to press matters to the length of a trial."

Sapin's reaction to his suggestion was not at all what Gautier had expected. Instead of looking sceptical or cautious, he grinned. "So you think she might, Inspector!"

"You don't seem surprised."

"Come, Inspector, let's not play games. You have already been told that the lady will not give evidence against me."

"It is not for the duchesse to decide whether you will be put on trial or not."

"The duchesse?"

"Yes. The Duchesse de Paiva. It was her necklace which we found in your possession."

Sapin's jaunty self-assurance seemed to evaporate. For a time he was silent as though he were reappraising the situation. Finally he said grudgingly: "What are these questions you wish me to answer?"

"For a start I'd like to know why you tried to steal that necklace."

"Why does a man steal?" Sapin's shrug of the shoulders showed he considered the question ridiculous.

"You would never be able to get rid of a necklace as well known as the duchesse's."

Gautier was by no means certain of his facts. He knew that many pieces of jewellery, tiaras, necklaces, bracelets, the great creations of Cartier and other famous craftsmen in precious stones, became well known the first time they were worn in public. Newspapers vied with each other in describing the gems from which they were made, their value, the beauty of the women who wore them and the wealth or the indiscretions of the men who bought them. Parisians were fascinated to learn that Comte Boni de Castellane, who in twelve years spent sixty million francs of his American wife's fortune, had bought two identical pearl necklaces, one for her and one for a little-known actress. They learned too that Otero, one of the most notorious cocottes in France, had been given a diamond corselet worth more than two million francs, and that when her rival, Liane de Pougy, visited Russia an astute Paris jeweller also made the journey, taking with him several fine pieces of his work, all of which were bought for Liane by Russian gentlemen who could not resist her beauty. Gautier could not remember ever having read of the Duchesse de Paiva's necklace but since she had been one of the best-known women of the demi-monde, it seemed safe to assume that it had been seen, admired and commented on by many people.

"I had reason to believe that the owner might be willing to buy it back," Sapin replied evasively.

"What I don't understand is why you should have even tried a trick like that. It isn't your style, Sapin."

"Sometimes a man feels like picking up a little easy money."

"The second thing I'd like to know," Gautier said, "is how you came by that invitation to the fête."

The invitation card which had been found on Sapin was in the drawer of Gautier's table. He took it out and looked at it. As far as one could tell the name inscribed on it had not been altered or defaced in any way.

"I've already told you. A man robbed a house in Neuilly and found the card there."

"Do you expect me to believe that you acquired the invitation by chance?"

"It's true. If you make enquiries you will learn that the man whose name is on the card, a Monsieur de Brissaude, left Paris several days ago."

There must be at least an element of truth in Sapin's story, Gautier decided. The facts he had given about the invitation could, if they were false, easily be disproved. Sapin had neither the imagination nor the nerve to plan a crime like the one he had essayed at the Tir aux Pigeons and the person who had put him up to it would almost certainly have provided him with a story that would stand up to investigation.

"We'll certainly check what you've told us," he said, "and if it is true I'll recommend to my superiors that you be released."

The policeman who had brought Sapin from jail to Gautier's office and who had been waiting at the back of the room during the interview, moved forward to take him away. Sapin allowed himself to be led out but he stopped at the door and looked at Gautier. Some of his self-confidence had returned.

"The lady has a very good reason for not wishing me to appear in court," he said.

"The Duchesse de Paiva? What reason?"

"She would not want all Paris to know that her necklace is worthless."

"Worthless? That's nonsense!"

"Take it from me, Inspector. The stones in the necklace are not genuine."

Gautier resisted the temptation to dismiss Sapin's story as invention. The thief had nothing to gain by lying at this stage. "How would you know?"

"As a young man I worked for two years in a jeweller's workshop, learning the trade." Sapin grinned. "Until temptation became too strong for me. Besides, in my business one has to know the value of jewellery or one is at the mercy of the receivers."

"In any case it's of no significance," Gautier said. "A good many ladies have copies of their jewellery made to wear on public occasions."

"Has the duchesse admitted the one she was wearing was a copy?"

Instead of replying Gautier nodded at the

policeman to take Sapin away. After they had left the room, he began writing a brief report for the Director of the Sûreté setting out the essential facts of what the Duchesse de Paiva had told him and concluding with a recommendation that Sapin should be released.

He had finished the report and was reading it through when Surat came into the room with a message for him. It was a "petit bleu" sent through the pneumatic system, a way of sending messages quickly and inexpensively much used by Parisians. Gautier opened the blue envelope and found that the message was from Madame de Saules. It read:

I am sorry that I felt unable to see you yesterday, Inspector, but I am free at 11.30 today and will be glad to see you then, if you would be good enough to call at my house.

Renée de Saules

Surat waited until Gautier had read the message and then he asked him: "Would you like me to arrange for a reply, Patron?"

"I sense that this is more of a command than an invitation," Gautier replied, "and an acceptance is not necessary. While I am gone, however, there is something else you can do."

"What's that?"

Gautier told him to find out whether a Monsieur Henri de Brissaude was named among the guests invited to Marie-Thérèse de Saules' party. If so, he should go to Neuilly where he might be able to learn whether Monsieur de Brissaude had left Paris and whether his home had been burgled.

"And seeing this message," Gautier added, holding up the petit bleu, "reminds me that you can send one for me. Telegraph the chief of police in Venice. I wish to know more about a Signor Daniele Pontana: in particular about his financial position, why he has left Italy to live in France and whether he has ever been in trouble with the authorities, for assault or violence, for example."

8

WHEN Madame de Saules received Gautier in her study at Rue du Bac, she was wearing a hat and carrying a parasol, as though she was ready to leave the house. He must have shown surprise, because she said at once: "I have to apologize for asking you to come and see me this morning, Inspector Gautier, because I now remember that I have another engagement."

"A pity, Madame, but it cannot be helped."

"Unfortunately the engagement is one which I must keep. Today is the anniversary of the death of Corinne Frèle, one of our most brilliant women writers. She died tragically a year ago and I agreed to lead a delegation from the Society of Women Writers to Passy this morning where we will place flowers on her grave."

"I can easily come again another time," Gautier told her.

"You're very kind. On the other hand if you

would accompany me to the cemetery this morning, we could talk on the way there."

"Willingly, Madame."

Madame de Saules began pulling on her gloves. It was clear she had never even considered the possibility that Gautier might not fall in with her suggestion. "Let us go then."

As they went downstairs together, Gautier glanced at her. She was a small woman, much smaller than the impression given by the portrait hanging in her study, who must have been strikingly attractive in her youth. Now, although neither her face nor her body showed any of the signs of age, one could detect in her eyes a weary recognition that life would never again offer her the pleasures or the excitement or the rewards that it had in the past.

When they reached the bottom of the stairs, they saw Marie-Thérèse. She was speaking to one of the servants and there was anger in her face and in her voice. The daughter of the house, Gautier had already decided, was not a girl who would readily tolerate anyone who did not carry out wishes promptly.

"Marie-Thérèse, don't forget that I'm

counting on you to be here for lunch," her mother called out.

"Lunch?"

"Yes. Some of our friends are coming back from the cemetery to lunch. I told you yesterday, remember."

"Oh, all right," Marie-Thérèse agreed grudgingly.

"Good. Otherwise we will be thirteen sitting down."

"I may have to leave before lunch is over. I have a riding lesson at three."

"Another lesson? That must be your second if not the third this week."

"I want to get in as many as I can before we leave for the country," Marie-Thérèse replied. Then she glanced at her mother and added: "If you're going to a funeral shouldn't you be wearing a veil?"

"It isn't a funeral," her mother replied. "And anyway I'm to make a speech."

A landau drawn by two chestnut horses stood in the courtyard of the house, the coachman on his box and a footman in livery standing waiting by the open door of the carriage. Madame de Saules and Gautier climbed in and the equipage moved off through the gateway into Rue du Bac and then turned north towards the Seine.

"You must be wondering why at her age my daughter is still taking riding lessons," Madame de Saules said suddenly.

"Why not, if she is fond of equestrianism?"

"Like all girls of good family Marie-Thérèse was taught to ride when she was a child, just as she was taught to draw, to play the pianoforte and to dance. She has a beautiful seat on a horse, but that's not enough. Not content with riding two or three times a week in the early mornings, she wants to be an expert and to do the kind of tricks one sees in circuses."

"Is there any harm in that?"

Madame de Saules did not give him a direct reply. Instead she continued moodily: "My husband should not have allowed it. It isn't decorous for a girl in her position. But he dotes on Marie-Thérèse and can refuse her nothing."

"Who is her teacher?" Gautier asked the question although intuition had already given him the answer.

"The Duchesse de Paiva."

The landau crossed the river by the Pont des Invalides and swung left towards Passy. A few idlers, mostly men in tightly buttoned suits and straw hats, were standing on the bridge looking down at the water. On the far side in the Cours la Reine, a horsedrawn omnibus had collided with a calèche. The accident did not appear to have been serious, but a small crowd had gathered to watch the omnibus driver and the coachman argue, while the two ladies who had been riding in the calèche stood some distance away, sheltering under their parasols and ignoring the vulgar scene.

"I'm sorry, Madame," Gautier said, "that yesterday I had to bring you the sad news of the abbé's death."

"It's monstrous! Unbelievable!" Madame de Saules exclaimed. "Is there no piety left in France, no respect for religion? How could anyone deliberately murder a priest?"

"It is difficult to understand, certainly."

"And how could anyone, even the most depraved villain, wish to kill a man as kind and gentle and Christian as Abbé Didier?"

The question, which he had already heard in the same or a different form several times, was beginning to irritate Gautier. He replied: "Unhappily, Madame, not everyone appears to have had such a high opinion of the abbé as you."

"What are you saying?" Madame de Saules demanded. "Has anyone spoken disparagingly of him to you?"

"Not disparagingly perhaps, but your daughter seems to have resented the way he interfered in her life."

Gautier's reply disconcerted Madame de Saules, as he had anticipated it might. Bluntness could sometimes shock people into revealing feelings which they would mask from tactful questioning. She said: "If Marie-Thérèse told you that it was only in a fit of petulance. Girls sometimes lose patience with their confessors."

"And was it also in a fit of petulance that she decided not to marry the Comte de Menilmont?"

He knew that the question risked an angry rebuff or a retort that her daughter's marriage was no business of the Sûreté, but Madame de Saules only shook her head in resignation. "You should be asking my husband these questions, Inspector."

"Why do you say that, Madame?"

"I have already told you that he can refuse her nothing. When she changed her mind about the marriage, he agreed. The question is who will marry her now."

"You think no one will?"

"Everyone in Paris knows the marriage had been arranged. She was obliged to honour the contract, morally if not in law. Tongues will be wagging and all kinds of reasons put forward to explain why the marriage fell through. It will be a brave man who is ready to risk being humiliated as the poor Comte de Menilmont was."

"Will she inherit from your husband?"

"Marie-Thérèse has already come into the money which her grandfather left to be hers on her eighteenth birthday. Eventually she will also inherit from us of course."

Gautier smiled. "In that case, Madame, she will never lack suitors."

"Yes. Adventurers and fortune hunters," Madame de Saules said scornfully.

"And you have no idea why she decided she no longer wished to marry the comte?"

"I suspect her decision may have been influenced by the Duchesse de Paiva."

Gautier knew she was wrong but he could not have said so without revealing that he had overheard the duchesse's conversation with

Marie-Thérèse at the Tir aux Pigeons. Instead he asked Madame de Saules: "Perhaps Abbé Didier advised her against the marriage?"

"Why on earth should he have done so?"

"The comte has a dubious reputation to say the least."

"That's just slanderous gossip." She paused and then said slowly, as though she were underlining her words for emphasis: "What passes in the confessional is of course secret, but I am absolutely certain that the abbé was strongly in favour of Marie-Thérèse marrying the comte and that he did his best to persuade her to do so.

They were passing the Palais de Trocadero and seconds later the Iandau drew to a halt outside the gates to the cemetery. Several people, mostly women, were passing through the gates and Madame de Saules and Gautier followed them. Inside a crowd had gathered around the grave of Corinne Frèle and Gautier noticed Monsieur de Saules among them. He smiled at his wife as she approached three other ladies who were evidently officers of the Society of Women Writers. One of the three was holding a large floral decoration of lilies and red roses, fashioned in the shape of a lyre.

While she and the three ladies were talking quietly, Gautier looked at Corinne Frèle's grave. Like most of the other graves in the cemetery it had an elaborate tombstone. Built of pink marble it was shaped like a small church, open at one end and with a tall gothic spire. Inside the church, beyond the head of the grave, was a stained-glass window on which had been painted within a border of lilies and roses, the epitaph which the poetess had written for herself before she died:

Life held her, trembling, in its cruel hand,
A prisoner to its passion and its pain,
Released at last, her soul flew skywards and
In kindly death found freedom once again.

Madame de Saules took the wreath, walked to the grave, turned towards the small crowd of mourners and began speaking. Her tribute to Corinne Frèle was beautifully phrased and lyrical, almost a masterpiece of prose in its own right. Gautier supposed that she had written it herself and then committed it to memory. She spoke of the dead writer's youth and promise, of the few fragile but exquisite poems she had

123

left as a testament to her talent, of her tragic death.

Among those who stood listening to Madame de Saules were several well known writers and poets; Judith, daughter of Théophile Gautier and the estranged wife of Catulle Mendès, Colette Willy whose novels with their heroine "Claudine" and their innuendoes of lesbian love had created a sensation, Renée Vivien, the English poet, lovely but melancholy, who seemed herself to be on the point of death.

When Madame de Saules finished her speech, she turned towards the tomb, knelt down in front of it for a few moments of prayer and crossed herself. She had performed the ceremony with simple dignity and without affectation or histrionics. Gautier was impressed and at the same time the sight of her kneeling by the poet's grave tugged at his memory but without response. She rose and returned to the other ladies. Her husband went to join her and presently the two of them came over to Gautier.

"May I congratulate you on your speech, Madame?" Gautier said. "It was very moving."

"Thank you."

While she had been carrying out the simple ceremony at the grave of Corinne Frèle,

Madame de Saules had seemed to recapture some of the animation with which, as a young vivacious girl, she had dazzled Paris society when, it was said, people listening to her frighteningly brilliant conversation had felt as though they were being battered by a hailstorm of diamonds. Now that her appearance in public was over, she appeared immediately to slip back into the sad, withdrawn loneliness of middle age.

"As you heard me tell my daughter," she told Gautier, "some of these ladies are lunching at our home today and two of them are riding with me to Rue du Bac. But my husband will be glad to take you to your office in his automobile."

"Thank you, but that really isn't necessary. I can easily find a fiacre or take the omnibus."

"No. No Inspector, I insist," Monsieur de Saules said. "The automobile is here and I am going in any case to my club in Rue Royale." He smiled. "I would be right out of my depth at a luncheon of literary ladies."

"Rue Royale would be very convenient as I have an errand to do in Rue St. Honoré."

Monsieur de Saules' automobile, the latest Dion-Bouton model, was standing outside the gates of the cemetery with a chauffeur on guard.

Automobiles were becoming more common in Paris, but they were still rare enough to draw a crowd and when they came to a halt in the street, people would press forward to touch them cautiously. In spite of the heat of the July day, the chauffeur wore leather leggings and gloves, a long motoring coat and a helmet.

"It's one of the front-engined models," Monsieur de Saules said, patting the automobile with an affection which showed that in spite of his wealth, he still found pleasure in a new possession.

The chauffeur started the engine and after a few noisy hiccoughs and a backfire which sent the spectators scampering, the Dion-Bouton moved off. Gautier recalled the only other previous occasion when he had ridden in an automobile. Monsieur Duclos, his father-in-law, an honest, hard-working bourgeois who had built up an excellent business selling china to the catering trade, used to take his two daughters and their husbands out to lunch every Sunday and once, on a quixotic impulse, he had hired two chauffeur-driven automobiles to take the family to eat in the countryside. The gesture had not been a success, for one of the automobiles had broken down and they had finished up lunching in an unprepossessing village café.

As they were driving along, Monsieur de Saules asked Gautier: "What has happened to that thief whom you arrested at my daughter's party?"

"Sapin? Nothing as yet. He will probably be released this afternoon."

"Are you saying he will not appear in court?"

"No. The Duchesse de Paiva does not want him to be put on trial."

The banker paused and then asked cautiously as though he were uncertain whether he wished to hear the answer to his question: "Did she give you any reason?"

"She believes it would cause your family embarrassment if it were known that a thief had managed to get into the Tir aux Pigeons and she does not wish to spoil your daughter's pleasure."

"How like her!" Monsieur de Saules exclaimed. "Really the woman is so kind and thoughtful, a saint! And of course she's devoted to Marie-Thérèse. They are like sisters."

"She was fortunate not to lose her necklace," Gautier remarked.

"We have your vigilance to thank for that."

"Still, I suppose at a function like that, with so many guests, she would not be wearing the real necklace, but a copy?"

The banker shook his head. "Prudence is completely foreign to Jeanne's nature. We've urged her frequently to have the necklace copied, but she has never done so."

The chauffeur stopped the automobile on the corner of Rue Royale and Rue St. Honoré to let Gautier alight. As he did so, Monsieur de Saules put out a hand to check him.

"Do you have any thoughts yet, Inspector, on who might have killed Abbé Didier?"

"Not as yet. We are still making enquiries."

"Would it help if I were to offer a sum of money to anyone who could assist in the scoundrel's capture?"

"A reward? They have used that idea in America, but I don't know whether it would work in France. Criminals in our country have a code of honour in which they take great pride."

"Well, the money is at your disposal if you need it. I had in mind twenty thousand francs, if that would be enough."

As three or four francs a day was a normal wage and even civil servants were often paid no more than 120 a month, twenty thousand francs would be a temptation stronger than all but the staunchest loyalty. "That should be ample," Gautier told Monsieur de Saules.

"My wife is not a vindictive woman," the banker said, "but it would please her to know that whoever killed the abbé did not escape punishment."

Heuze, the jeweller in Rue St. Honoré, received Gautier with dignified courtesy. A man whose clients included King Leopold of Belgium and the Shah of Persia did not need to be obsequious, nor had Heuze any reason to be afraid of the police. Gautier had visited the shop before, when he was making enquiries about Josephine Hassler, a former mistress of the President of France who was suspected of having murdered her husband. The jeweller had given Gautier very helpful information about the jewellery of Madame Hassler, but it did not seem as though he were going to be so co-operative in the matter of the Duchesse de Paiva's necklace.

"Clients come to my establishment, Inspector," he said when he had heard what it was Gautier wished to know, "in preference to one of the famous jewellers, because they know they can rely on my discretion."

"And you, Monsieur, can rely on mine."

"Is the duchesse's necklace the subject of criminal proceedings?"

"A man attempted to steal it but we caught him. At the request of the duchesse he is not to be put on trial."

"Then why, may I ask, are you making these enquiries?"

"To satisfy myself."

Heuze toyed with the heavy gold watchchain which he wore looped across his waistcoat, as he tried to decide whether the ethics of his profession were worth more than the goodwill of the police. Finally he said: "You must understand, Inspector, that the Duchesse de Paiva has never been one of my clients, but the high-class jewellers of Paris are a small and friendly fraternity. We exchange information among ourselves, in confidence naturally, for our own protection. I know the name of the jeweller who made the diamond and sapphire necklace, the name of the man who bought it and how much he paid for it."

"None of these things interest me."

"Then what is it you wish to know?"

"Are you aware if a copy was ever made of the necklace?"

Heuze's hesitation was momentary, that of a man who wished to choose his words with care. "As it happens I know about that too. A jeweller named Lianchy, a good friend of mine and an excellent craftsman, was asked to copy it only a short time ago."

"Would one be able to tell immediately that the stones were not real?"

"A jeweller could tell at a glance," Heuze replied, with the satisfaction of one who took pride in his craft, "but a copy by Lianchy, even though he was obliged to make this particular one in a very short space of time, would be good enough to deceive anyone who had no knowledge of stones."

"I see."

"Unless of course they were very close indeed to the duchesse." He smiled. Now that he had told Gautier what he knew, he could enjoy the luxury of a modest joke. "And they tell me she's not as approachable as she once was."

"I wonder then," Gautier said thoughtfully, "why she should conceal the fact that she had a copy of the necklace from her friends."

Heuze stopped smiling and he said slowly: "Perhaps, Inspector, a copy is all that she has."

"Are you suggesting that she has disposed of the real necklace?"

"She sold it only the other day."

9

DANIELE PONTANA was living in an apartment in Rue du Cherche-Midi which scarcely seemed equal to his manner and style of life. It was immediately above a baker's shop and it shared with the apartments above it a door from the street, a narrow hallway and a dark, winding staircase with a stone floor. The staircase smelt not of freshly baked bread, but of the nameless, unpleasant smells of age and decay that accumulate in an old building.

As he climbed the stairs, Gautier thought about the message which had arrived by telegraph from the police in Venice and which he had brought with him in his pocket. It read:

From: Chief of Police, Venezia.
To: Sûreté, Parigi.
We repeat Pontana arrested twice. First time charged with abducting Francesca, daughter of Duca di Ligorno. Charges dropped at request of girl's parents and couple

subsequently married. Arrested again in Bologna together with Contessa Donatella di Rinzo on charge of adultery brought by Contessa's husband. Both found guilty and sentenced to six months in prison but released immediately on a technicality and then pardoned. Pontana's financial difficulties his reason for leaving Italy and several civil lawsuits await him should he return. No proven offences of violence.

Gautier realized that the Italian's financial problems must account for his comparatively humble style of life in Paris. Even so if, as one assumed, he was receiving no income from Italy, someone must be supporting him and Gautier wondered whether, as Juliette had suggested, it was a mistress.

The door of the apartment was opened by a man of about forty who introduced himself as Enrico Ponzi, the private secretary of Daniele Pontana. Ponzi had a complexion almost dark enough to be mistaken for an African, but his features were unmistakably those of a man from the far south of Europe.

After explaining who he was, Gautier said: "I

have come to ask Signor Pontana some questions."

"I regret, Monsieur, that he is not at home."

"Perhaps you as his secretary may be able to tell me what I wish to know and thus save me from troubling your employer."

"Is it about money?" Ponzi asked anxiously.

"No. What I have come to discuss has no connection with Signor Pontana's financial difficulties."

"In that case, Monsieur, please come in."

The living room of the apartment had been decorated in an Italian style with a floor of dark green tiles on which lay two tiger skins, heavy Renaissance furniture and two small but exquisite paintings, which Gautier guessed might have been the work of seventeenth-century artists. The central feature of the room was a large portrait, executed in the manner of Paolo Veronese, in which Pontana was pictured in Renaissance costume. The effect was to make him appear neither heroic nor romantic but faintly absurd.

"I can see that Signor Pontana's finances are a source of anxiety for you," Gautier remarked after they had both sat down.

"Anxiety! They are a perpetual nightmare! If

only they worried him as much as they trouble me!"

"He spends freely then?"

"Regrettably he was born with the tastes of a nobleman, a prince." Ponzi pointed towards a door which must lead to the poet's bedroom. "Through there he has more than sixty suits and an equal number of pairs of shoes. And yet tomorrow, should he happen to pass a shirt-maker's establishment, he will go in and be measured for twenty shirts of an expensive silk that takes his fancy."

"And it is your task to find the money to pay all these bills?"

"Precisely." Ponzi's French was fluent but unlike that of his employer, heavily accented. Gautier thought he could recognize in it a resemblance to the harsh accent of the Midi in France, which made him think Ponzi might come from the equivalent region in Italy, the Mezzogiorno.

"Is it true that Signor Pontana had to leave Italy because he was being harassed by creditors?"

"There's no point in denying it. Yes, hounded by bailiffs, showered with writs, he was quite unable to work. A poet needs serenity, peace of mind."

"But wouldn't his wife's family help him? I had heard she comes of a rich, aristocratic Venetian family."

"Rich and aristocratic they may be, but they treated him miserably even when she was alive."

"Are you telling me that Signora Pontana is dead?"

"Yes. She died three months ago."

"I had always understood he still had a wife."

"People in France have not heard of her death." Ponzi looked at Gautier like a man who wonders whether what he is about to say will be believed. Then he added: "Signor Pontana felt it would be wiser if those he met in Paris still thought he was a married man."

"I wonder why."

"He has always been attractive to women. Many of them pursue him quite shamelessly. If it were known that he were unattached, his life would become intolerable."

"I see." Gautier nodded, resisting the temptation to laugh at the notion of Pontana sheltering modestly from the advances of a legion of women.

On the wall of the room facing them hung a small collection of antique weapons; a medieval foot-soldier's pike, two crossed broadswords, a sabre with a jewelled scabbard and a set of five daggers. The daggers were a matched set, identical in shape and embellishment and mounted in gradation of size on a fan-shaped wooden rack. Recalling the Comte de Menilmont's remarks about Pontana's skill in swordsmanship, Gautier half expected to see in the room another portrait of the Italian, poised ready for a duel, épée in hand.

"As long as his daughter was alive," Ponzi continued, "the Duca di Ligorno at least helped her with enough money to stop her husband's creditors from taking him to court. He did not want another scandal, one supposes. But once she was dead the family abandoned him, which is really the reason he came to France."

"And is no one helping him with money at all now?" Gautier asked, leaving the secretary to interpret the question in whatever way he chose.

"As to that, you will have to ask Signor Pontana himself," Ponzi said stiffly, aware perhaps that he had been speaking too freely. "You are asking all these questions, Monsieur, but you still have not told me the purpose of your visit. You said it was not connected with financial matters."

"That's right. It isn't. I am here because we are making enquiries into the killing of a local priest, the Abbé Didier."

"A priest has been killed? You mean assassinated?"

The question seemed genuine enough. Gautier realized that a foreigner who did not read French newspapers nor listen to local gossip might well not have heard about the abbé's death.

"Regrettably, yes."

"But how could that concern Signor Pontana?"

"He was acquainted with the abbé."

"I think you must be mistaken, Monsieur."

"What makes you think that?"

Ponzi shook his head, in sorrow it seemed. "Monsieur Gautier, I am a good Catholic and have been all my life. So you can imagine how it grieves me to tell you that Signor Pontana has been fighting the Church ever since he was a boy. He has no friends among the clergy."

"Why should that be?"

"He scorns priests and Catholic orthodoxy. I

suppose one might trace his attitude back to the days when he was educated at a Jesuit college. Daniele was the most brilliant and the most precocious student the college had ever taught. He learnt easily, quickly and with a prodigious appetite. By the age of fourteen he could write better Greek and Latin prose and verse than his teachers, had mastered French and as for philosophy, he could hold his own in disputation with anyone."

"And he began to believe he knew more than his professors?"

"Yes. But more than that, he decided that he was above their discipline and the petty regulations of the school. At thirteen he seduced the daughter of the school cook, a great strapping big-breasted peasant of nineteen as he described her. Any other boy at the place would have been expelled with ignominy, but he knew the principal could never bear to lose the pupil who everyone believed was going to bring the school glory and fame."

"And you say he has been in trouble with the Church since then as well," Gautier remarked.

"Frequently. His books have been proscribed, his way of life and his politics condemned from the pulpit. He has attacked the Church in his writing and in speeches and has even been threatened with the supreme penalty."

"You mean excommunication?"

"Yes."

Gautier decided that, loyal and conscientious though he might be, Ponzi was not an intelligent man. Even now he seemed not to have realized the purpose of Gautier's visit and everything he was saying about his master's antagonism towards the Church might have been construed as a motive for killing Abbé Didier.

"We know that your employer knew the abbé who was killed," he told Ponzi, "because he was overheard quarrelling with him in his church only a few days ago."

The secretary looked at him with horror. "Does that mean you suspect Signor Pontana of murdering this priest?"

"Not necessarily. We are speaking with everyone who might possibly have had a reason for killing the abbé."

"You must be mad! It is inconceivable that he would raise his hand against a priest. He is a Catholic."

"But you yourself said he is on the worst of terms with the clergy."

Ponzi came to a sudden decision. He said brusquely: "Inspector, I know nothing of this. You must speak with Signor Pontana himself."

"Indeed, I wish to do so. Do you know where I can find him?"

"No. I have no idea."

"Then are you expecting him to be home shortly?"

"No. That is I don't know when he will return. Possibly not till very late tonight." Ponzi could not conceal his growing agitation. "And now, Inspector, you must excuse me. I have work to do."

Gautier allowed himself to be shown out of the apartment and went downstairs. A hundred metres or so along the street a line of fiacres stood waiting. He walked past them, crossed the street and stationed himself in the shadow of a building where he would not be seen by anyone leaving Pontana's apartment. He did not have long to wait. In less than five minutes Ponzi came out of the door next to the baker's shop, hurried towards the line of fiacres and climbed into the first one he reached. The coachman cracked his whip and the fiacre moved off northwards towards Rue de Grenelle.

Crossing the street, Gautier took the next

fiacre and told the driver to follow the one in which Ponzi had left. The Italian's agitation on hearing of Pontana's quarrel with Abbé Didier and the haste with which he had left the apartment as soon as Gautier had gone, suggested that he might be going to warn his employer of the enquiries that the Sûreté was making. Gautier, for no good reason except curiosity, wished to see where he would go.

As the two fiacres, a respectable distance apart, crossed Rue de Grenelle, turned left on reaching Boulevard St. Germain and headed towards the river, he thought about what he had learned of Pontana from the telegraph message received from Venice and from what Ponzi had said. Although there appeared to be nothing in the poet's past to show that he was disposed towards violence, he was plainly a man who, when pursuing something he wanted, could be ruthless, determined and entirely without scruples.

After crossing the Seine to the Right Bank, the fiacre in which Ponzi was travelling passed through the Place de la Concorde and turned into Avenue des Champs Elysées. Children from well-to-do families were bowling their hoops in the gardens which bordered the avenue under the protective gaze of their governesses. The fiacre passed them and the Rond Point before drawing up in front of the entrance to a large house.

Gautier's fiacre also stopped and he watched thoughtfully from a distance as Ponzi got down and walked through the gates of the house. As most Parisians would have done, he recognized both the house and the fine coach, upholstered in yellow and drawn by four splendid black horses, which stood waiting outside it. Both the house and the equipage belonged to the Duchesse de Paiva.

10

THE smell of incense lingered in the church of Sainte Clothilde, a reminder of countless masses for the dead, for departed souls, for anniversaries still remembered. Gautier almost fancied that he could see it, suspended in the damp, musty air of the church, heightening the gloom till one could scarcely distinguish the flickering lights of the candles which burned by the statue of the Virgin.

His footsteps echoed as he walked up one side of the church to the chapel of Sainte Clothilde. The hand-written notice attached to the railings which separated the chapel from the main body of the church and which had read "Monsieur l''Abbé hears confessions every weekday between 6.30 and 7.30" had been hastily corrected by pasting a slip of paper bearing the words "le Curé" over the words "l'Abbé".

Two people were sitting in the chapel waiting their turn to enter the confessional. One was a girl, probably no older than seventeen although she looked thirty, whose drawn cheeks and thin, brittle body suggested consumption. The other was the woman who had been in the church on the day the abbé was killed and who had found his body.

He had wakened even earlier than usual that morning and, walking to the Sûreté by a circuitous route to pass the time, had decided on an impulse to go into the church. At the back of his mind was a faint hope that he might notice something in or around the chapel which had escaped his notice on his previous visit and which might have a bearing on the abbé's death.

He walked slowly round the church. Ringed in a semi-circle beyond the main altar were a number of chapels dedicated to other saints, each of which had one or two confessionals, though none were in use at the time. On the far side of the church, directly opposite the chapel of Sainte Clothilde, was another similar in size and shape, dedicated to Saint Valère. Further down towards the entrance of the church was the pulpit, perched above the congregation and reached by twin flights of wooden stairs. It was crowned with its own wooden canopy, which had an imitation gothic spire. Gautier supposed that it was from the pulpit that Abbé Didier had preached to his congregation, directing their steps to the path which would lead, if not to righteousness, then at least to a better life.

When he had been right around the church and reached the chapel of Sainte Clothilde again, the consumptive girl was coming out of the confessional and the other woman had just taken her place. Gautier sat down in one of the chairs in the main body of the church to wait until she re-emerged. As only two days had passed since she had last been to confession, he assumed she did so regularly and that the curé was unlikely to detain her for long and he was right. She came out, knelt briefly in front of the altar of the chapel and as she began shuffling towards the other side of the church, he intercepted her.

After he had reminded her of their previous meeting, he said: "Do you come to the church often at this time of the morning, Madame?"

"Every day."

"Not to confess, surely?"

"Of course not!" Her tone made it clear that the police had no business to be prying into matters of spiritual conscience. "I come to help in the church, to do a little cleaning, throw

147

away dead flowers, replenish the stocks of candles."

"Excellent! Then you are just the person to help me find out who killed the abbé."

The woman looked at him more tolerantly. "If I can help, Inspector, then of course I shall."

"Then tell me, did you see anyone unusual in the church when you were here in the mornings? Before the abbé was killed, I mean."

"In what way unusual?"

"Someone you would not expect to find here at that hour."

"Only the lady in the veil."

"What lady was that?"

"The same one I saw leaving the church on the day the abbé was killed."

"You did not tell me she was wearing a veil."

The woman shrugged her shoulders. "You never asked me what she was wearing and anyway it's what you would expect from a lady coming to confession so early in the morning."

"Let me understand you," Gautier said. "Are you saying you had seen her here before?"

"Yes."

Gautier realized that the fault had been his. He had not questioned the woman as thoroughly as he should have done, forgetting that the shock of finding a priest dead would have stifled even a Frenchwoman's talkativeness.

"When had you seen her previously?" he asked the woman.

"She was here a day or two before I found the abbé dead, sitting in the chapel, waiting her turn for confession."

"Can you remember which day it was?"

Her face puckered up in a grimace of concentration, but she shook her head. "No. One day is very much like another for me, except for Sundays of course."

"What made you notice her?"

"Her clothes. As I have already told you, she was dressed like a lady and ladies don't often come here to confess and certainly never at that hour of the morning."

"Did she actually make a confession?"

"I suppose so. Why else would she have been here? I didn't wait to see her go into the confessional, for another woman went in immediately after me."

"And was that the only other time you had seen this person?"

"No. Once before I had seen her coming out

of the sacristy in the middle of the morning. She must have been to see the abbé. He was always there between eleven and twelve for any parishioner who wished to speak to him."

"What day was that?"

"I cannot be sure."

"Are you certain it was the same woman?"

She shrugged her shoulders again. "As I said, she was wearing a veil, but it isn't very likely that another like her would be coming to the church. Mostly ladies expect the abbé to go and see them."

"Did she wear the same clothes on every occasion?"

"Both times I saw her in the early morning she wore a dark grey dress, a black hat and veil."

"What about the day when you saw her coming out of the sacristy?"

"No. That time she was dressed differently. I think she wore a blue dress."

Gautier asked her a few more questions, hoping that they might help to crystallize some half-forgotten fact or detail that lay in her memory, but she appeared to know nothing more that might help him. So he thanked her for her help and she went away to carry out some of her daily duties on the far side of the church. He sat down on one of the chairs in the chapel of Sainte Clothilde and waited for Father Xavier.

After a few minutes the priest, deciding evidently that he could expect no more penitents that morning, came out of the confessional. When he saw Gautier sitting there, he hesitated as though uncertain as to what he should do.

"It's all right, Father," Gautier said, "I've come on police business, not on the Lord's."

"You wish to see me, Inspector?"

"That was not really why I came. I wanted to speak with the woman who was here on the morning the abbé was killed. She works in the church, I believe."

"Oh, yes, you must mean Madame Berthe. Was she able to help you?"

"Perhaps."

Gautier told him what the woman had said about the lady in the veil she had seen in the church. Then he asked the priest: "Have you ever seen a woman of that description, Father?"

Father Xavier shook his head. "No lady of quality would come to the church at that hour of the morning and alone."

"Then you have no idea who she might be?"

"No," the priest agreed and then added thoughtfully: "Unless of course . . . but there is probably no connection."

"What is it, Father?"

"I recall a remark the abbé once made."

Father Xavier went on to explain that the curates of the parish sometimes teased Abbé Didier for continuing to spend so much time in the church every morning, even when nobody came to confess. They used to compare him jokingly with anglers who spent all day by the river but caught nothing. The abbé used to smile and say that he was a fisher of men.

"One morning a few days ago," Father Xavier continued, "when he came back for breakfast, we asked him as usual what his catch had been that morning. He told us two fishes but one had got away. When we asked what he meant, he said that another woman had come and actually knelt down in the confessional, but that when he had drawn the shutter back, she rose and hurried away. He thought she had come intending to make a confession but that at the last minute her courage had failed her."

"Does that happen often?"

"Not very often. Usually only when a person has a very great sin to confess."

"A sin like murder, perhaps?"

As they had been talking they had walked through the church together, around the back of the altar and past the other small chapels. When they reached the door to the sacristy, they stopped.

"We are holding a requiem mass for the abbé tomorrow morning," Father Xavier told Gautier. "Will you come, Inspector?"

"If my duties allow it, yes Father."

As he walked towards the main doors of the church, Gautier thought about his own spiritual life. When Suzanne and he were together they went to Mass every Sunday, except when he was on duty, sometimes with her parents. Since she had left him he had been once or twice, but had found himself unable to concentrate on the liturgy and the act of praying seemed unreal. He did not search his conscience nor blame himself for his neglect of religion, but recognized it as though he were a detached observer studying his own behaviour.

Madame Berthe was working near the church doors, cleaning brasswork. When she saw Gautier, she came to meet him. She said:

"There's one other thing I remember, Inspector."

"Oh, yes?"

"On the day the lady in the veil came out of the sacristy, I left the church at the same time as she did. I was going home."

"And what happened?"

"A carriage was waiting for her; a big carriage, yellow and black, with four black horses, a coachman and two footmen."

Later that morning when Surat came into his room, Gautier saw at once that the man was worried. They had been working together for over two years now and Surat had proved himself to be physically courageous and in most circumstances imperturbable. At the same time he had a weakness, which it would be unfair to call moral cowardice. He was afraid of the wrath of his superiors, of reprimands, of humiliation, of disgrace.

"I have to tell you, Patron, that there is likely to be trouble."

"What kind of trouble?"

"It has to do with my report. Did you read it?"

"Yes. It was excellent."

The report which Gautier had found waiting for him when he arrived at the Sûreté from the church of Sainte Clothilde, gave the results of the enquiries which Surat had made the previous afternoon into the invitation card found in Emil Sapin's possession. He had been able to establish that a Monsieur Henri de Brissaude was on the list of guests invited to the ball at the Tir aux Pigeons. The secretary of Monsieur de Saules had received a petit bleu accepting the invitation. It was an unconventional way to reply to a formal invitation but Monsieur de Brissaude was known to be a bachelor and therefore an eccentric. The police at Neuilly had confirmed that de Brissaude had left Paris for the summer and they had received a report that his house had been broken into, but apparently nothing of value had been stolen.

In general the report was very much what Gautier had expected, confirming Sapin's story. It was only in the last sentence that Surat had produced the unexpected. He had discovered that de Brissaude was a cousin of Madame Geneviève Trocville.

"I didn't confine my enquiries to Neuilly," Surat said.

"What else did you do?"

"I visited a café near Avenue Hoche and struck up a conversation with one of Madame Trocville's servants."

"And did you learn anything?"

"No," Surat confessed and his embarrassment was painful. "Now Madame Trocville has come to complain."

"How do you know that?"

"She is in the waiting-room downstairs with her husband. They have demanded to see the Director."

"Don't worry about it. I can deal with anything the lady may have to say."

Surat left the room, still upset and still worried. Gautier could only feel sympathy for him. The man had gone beyond the strict letter of his instructions, using his initiative as a good police officer should, but had achieved nothing. The same thing had happened to Surat more than once before. Was it simply bad luck or was this the fundamental reason why he had never reached senior rank? Could there be some flaw in a man's judgement which made him susceptible to bad timing? Gautier had not found an answer to the question when

Courtrand's personal assistant arrived to tell him that the Director wished to see him.

Monsieur and Madame Trocville were seated in the Director's spacious office and Courtrand was pacing the floor, an unpromising sign. Whenever he was really angry, he walked up and down in front of his desk, more often than not with his hands clasped behind his back. It may have been that, as a small man, he subconsciously needed to reinforce his authority by looking down on the people to whom he was speaking and whom he usually kept seated during these displays.

"I sent for you, Inspector," he said loudly as soon as Gautier came into the room, "because this lady and gentleman have a serious complaint to make."

"I am sorry to hear that, Monsieur le Directeur."

"Monsieur Trocville is a man of good standing. His brother is the deputy for the Loiret. It is intolerable that his family should be exposed to such treatment. No doubt you have an explanation?"

"He will not be able to give an explanation that will satisfy me!" Monsieur Trocville declared indignantly.

Gautier could not remember seeing Monsieur Trocville at his wife's soirée earlier in the week. He was a lean man, whose hunched shoulders, tufted white eyebrows and long nose gave him the look of a predatory bird. In spite of this he did not give the impression of being by nature bombastic or aggressive.

"Would it help if I were to know the nature of the complaint?" Gautier edged his words with an irony so delicate that he knew it would escape Courtrand.

"It seems that your assistant Surat has been making enquiries about Madame Trocville and her family in the neighbourhood of their home."

"Enquiries! He has been cross-examining our servants about our movements and our relatives. Anyone might think we were common criminals! Whoever he is I insist that he be dismissed."

"Was Surat acting on your instructions?" Courtrand asked Gautier.

"Yes." In a court of law, Gautier decided, his lie could be defended as the truth. Surat had been acting on his instructions, although not following them.

"I have to take the gravest view of this,"

Courtrand said pompously. "The matter will not be left here."

"My brother will raise it with the Prefect of Police, you can be assured of that."

"You are supposed to be investigating the death of Abbé Didier. What possible connection can Madame Trocville have with that affair?"

"None."

"Is that all you have to say?"

Gautier noticed that Madame Trocville had not so far spoken. She sat upright in her chair, looking sometimes at her husband and sometimes at Courtrand but never at Gautier, as though she were afraid that a single glance might provoke him into saying things which she did not wish to hear. He decided that the time had come to put her out of her misery.

"The enquiries Surat has been making did not concern the abbé's death," he said calmly, "or only indirectly. He was looking into the events which led to the theft of the Duchesse de Paiva's necklace."

"What on earth are you talking about?"

"Sapin was supposed to steal Madame's necklace." Gautier nodded towards Madame Trocville. "He did not know her by sight, but he had been given a description of the dress she would be wearing; a striking dress which could not be mistaken, but unfortunately the Duchesse de Paiva came to the ball in an identical dress."

"Is this man mad?" Trocville asked Courtrand. "What is all this talk of necklaces?"

"It had been arranged that Sapin would steal Madame's necklace and that it would be bought back from him for an agreed sum. That was to be his payment."

"Mother of God!" Courtrand shouted in exasperation. "Why would anyone invent a mad scheme like that?"

"To ruin the party and to humiliate the de Saules family. It was to be a revenge for past wrongs, an act in a long-standing feud."

The indignation on Trocville's face slowly vanished, to be replaced first by suspicion and then by dismay. He looked at his wife and she looked away, like a small girl caught out in a deceitful act.

"I still do not understand," Courtrand said almost plaintively. "Who is supposed to have engineered this conspiracy?"

"Why not ask Madame?"

The three men looked at Madame Trocville. Her lips were quivering as though she had something to say but could not find the words and her eyes had the look of a hunted animal. When at last she did speak, it was as though a dam had burst and the sentences came out, tumbling and beyond control.

"Why look at me? I know nothing of this man Sapin. Madame de Saules and I may not be the closest of friends, but it's ridiculous to suggest that I would wish to spoil her daughter's birthday. What reason have you for accusing me of hiring Sapin to steal my necklace? Just because he got into the Tir aux Pigeons with Henri's invitation? That was stolen when Henri's house was burgled." She stopped abruptly, but too late, realizing what she had said.

"How did you know it was Monsieur de Brissaude's invitation that Sapin used?" Gautier asked quietly.

"I was told so," she replied hastily, improvising. "I don't remember by whom. It must have been Monsieur de Saules. Yes, I'm sure it was he."

Her husband stood up. "Geneviève, my dear, we have taken up enough of these gentlemen's time." He offered her his arm and Gautier could only admire his dignity as he bowed slightly, first to Courtrand and then to him. "Monsieur le Directeur, Monsieur l'Inspecteur, I apologize for the trouble we have caused you."

11

THE Cirque Alfredi was one of the largest of the many circuses in Paris, second only in size to L'Hippodrome and considered by many to be superior for the quality of the acts it offered and the professionalism of its performers. Instead of the classic, circular ring, it had a rectangular arena, more than 130 metres long, while behind the scenes were stables for 50 horses and 20 elephants, as well as cages to hold 100 wild animals. More than 8,000 spectators could be accommodated in the seats that were ranged on three sides of the arena, while the wealthy and privileged could watch the spectacle from the comfort of twenty private boxes at the back.

When she had invited him to go to the circus, the Duchesse de Paiva had given Gautier one of her visiting cards, on the back of which she had written a brief introduction to the management of the Alfredi. When he had arrived there, Gautier had shown the card at the entrance and had been taken to the duchesse's box with a deference that bordered on servility. In spite of her humble origins in the circus, or perhaps because of them, the duchesse was clearly held in the highest esteem at the Alfredi.

Although the performance was due to start in less than five minutes, there was only one person in the box which could seat a dozen in comfort. It was Juliette Prévot and her expression when she saw Gautier was a blend of suspicion and annoyance.

Instead of returning Gautier's greeting she said shortly: "I suppose you arranged this to have another opportunity of cross-questioning me."

"I had no idea you were going to be here," Gautier replied.

"In that case why are you here? You're not a friend of the duchesse, as far as I know."

"She felt that I had done her a small service and to show her gratitude invited me to join her party here tonight."

He sat down next to her. For two people occupying a box to sit apart would have looked absurd. "And you? Are you fond of circuses?" he asked Juliette.

"I was brought up with horses and I love them. Jeanne sometimes invites me here when she is trying to make up a party, because she knows I'll always come."

Although the circus was essentially a popular form of entertainment, one could always find any number of men from society among the spectators. Horsemanship and a knowledge of horses had for centuries been considered one of the prerogatives of the aristocracy and the tradition had survived all the revolutions of the past 120 years. Many of the men who went to the circus, however, were more interested in the lady riders who were generally accepted as being as beautiful and as desirable as the ballet dancers of the Opéra. Jeanne Baroche was only one of many circus riders who had either married into society or been set up as the mistress of a marquis or a banker. Céleste Mogador became the Comtesse de Chabrillan, while Emilie Loisset, Marguerite Dudlay and Lina Imperia had all in their time won the hearts of wealthy men. Not surprisingly, society ladies did not approve of this vulgar traffic in beauty and Gautier could well understand that the Duchesse de Paiva might have difficulty in finding many who would join her in her box on Thursday evenings.

"If there is to be a party of us," Gautier remarked, "where are the others?"

"Jeanne only ever comes to see the second half of the performance," Juliette replied. "She says that acrobats and performing animals bore her."

She and Gautier watched the first half of the programme together. Almost all of the acts were by acrobats of one kind or another, balancing on wire, swinging on trapezes or forming human pyramids. In between the main turns were shorter interludes; a strong man bent iron bars, tumblers jumped through paper hoops, clowns threw water at each other.

As soon as the show began, Juliette's mood of truculence seemed to disappear. She watched the acts with the same fascination that Gautier could see on the faces of children among the audience. The daring of the trapeze artists somersaulting as they swung through the air made her gasp and more than once she reached out involuntarily to grab Gautier's arm.

The last act before the interval was one in which performing elephants were used in a parody of a tiger hunt, supposedly by Englishmen in India. Two men in white shorts and pith helmets, accompanied by two turbanned

166

maharajahs, rode on the elephants and were continually frustrated in their efforts to shoot the tigers stalking below them by the tricks of the elephants which trumpeted, reared up on their hind legs, knelt down without warning and from time to time sprayed the hunters with water from their trunks. With memories of Fashoda and imagined slights of diplomacy still fresh, the French were enjoying one of their periodic moods of anglophobia and this mocking of their imperialist neighbours delighted the audience as the first half of the show drew to a close.

When the last of the animals lurched out of the arena, Juliette turned towards Gautier. "The interval lasts for half an hour," she told him, "to give the audience time to look at the animals in their cages."

"Do you want to go and see them?"

"Yes, I'd like to. My father often took me to the circus when I was a little girl and we always made a point of going to see the animals. There you find the real atmosphere of the circus."

Leaving the box, they made their way to the far end of the building beyond the entrance through which the performers had come into the arena, where the stables and cages were to be found. To create an atmosphere of primitive savagery, the menagerie was poorly lit by oil lamps with here and there flaming torches placed so that they threw grotesque shadows over the walls and across the cages. The air was heavy with the smell of animals and sawdust and dung.

Seeing the naked flames of the torches, Gautier remembered that not many years previously the Cirque Molier had been burnt to the ground. Fortunately the circus had been empty at the time but the fire had come only a few months after a much more serious conflagration when the building in which the annual Bazar de la Charité was being held had been destroyed. More than 140 people from Paris society, mostly ladies, had been burned alive.

Instinctively Gautier offered his arm to Juliette, realizing too late that she would in all probability scorn a protective gesture from a man. To his surprise she took it and they threaded their way through the crowds, stopping at the cages of the lions and tigers and for a longer time at the stables to look at the horses.

"Do you know the Duchesse de Paiva well?" Gautier asked Juliette as they walked.

"I suppose no one could say we were intimate

friends. She often invites me to her house, usually when she needs a single woman to make up her numbers."

"Are there many literary and artistic people among her friends?"

Entertaining at the duchesse's house, Gautier reasoned, could not conform strictly to the protocol usually observed by society if she invited an unattached woman to her house. Single women would only accept an invitation to a social function if they were properly chaperoned and a divorced woman had no standing at all. It was only in literary salons that Juliette Prévot would be accepted in her own right as an authoress.

"You may think it surprising, but the answer is yes. One cannot help but admire Jeanne. She was born in the humblest circumstances, the daughter of a gipsy dancer in a troupe of itinerant fairground players. As she was given no education she was illiterate till the age of eighteen. Since that time she has not only taught herself to read and write, but studied literature and the arts. Her culture may have been late in developing, but it is genuine."

"She appears to be very friendly with Marie-Thérèse de Saules."

Juliette looked at him sharply. "What is the innuendo behind that remark?"

"I meant no innuendo at all."

"Have you added her to your list of suspects in the Didier affair?" The question was prickly with indignation.

"I have no list of suspects."

"I suppose you've decided that because she does not belong to tout Paris, because she was a circus performer and a cocotte, that she's the most likely person to have killed a priest."

"Not at all."

"Who are you to pass moral judgements on her? She has the right to take whomever she chooses for her lover and if she loves a man what is more natural than that she should wish to be a friend of his daughter?"

Gautier looked at her in surprise. "What are you saying?"

"Are you telling me that you didn't know?" Juliette asked incredulously. "Jeanne has been the mistress of Monsieur de Saules for the past five years."

When they returned to their seats, they found that the rest of the duchesse's party had arrived. The other guests were the couple whom Juliette and Gautier had met at Madame Trocville's reception, Monsieur and Madame Borde, a Portuguese named Vieira and his wife, distant cousins of the former Duc de Paiva and Comte Raymond de Menilmont.

"You haven't been to look at the animals, surely!" Madame Borde exclaimed.

"Yes," Juliette replied, "I always go."

"But even if it's safe it must be disgustingly dirty."

"What did you think of the horses?" asked the comte.

"They are superb."

"My ancestor the Marquis de Chinanville, who led Louis XIV's finest cavalry regiments, was accepted to be the finest horseman of his time, perhaps of any age."

"Earlier this week," the Portuguese Vieira said, "Monsieur Colchart showed me his stable at Auteuil. He has a wonderful string of horses, the best I've ever seen, especially one particularly fine Arab stallion."

"Is that the Colchart who owns the Nouveau Prix store?" Borde asked.

"Yes."

"I have no doubt his horses cost him a great deal of money," de Menilmont said. "But that's what is wrong with the world today. The wrong people have the wealth. Money should only be spent by people of taste and good judgement. It should be spent on enriching life, on protecting our national heritage, on fine art and rare books and on arranging for musicians of talent to perform great music. But the vast fortunes of today belong to the shopkeepers and soap manufacturers and railroad magnates." The comte, Gautier was certain, was about to add bankers to his list of the nouveau riche, but checked himself just in time. Instead he said: "Riches they may have but what can such people possibly know about how riches should be spent?"

"I hope you're not including me in your strictures," the Duchesse de Paiva said lightly.

"Certainly not, Madame. You have always spent your money wisely. The pictures, the porcelain and furniture in your house are exquisite." The comte smiled as he added: "But then, you have had the good taste to seek my advice."

The discussion on aesthetics and money was cut short as the second half of the circus programme began with a fanfare of trumpets. A team of four lady riders mounted on white horses came in and performed a display which combined athletic horsemanship with superbly disciplined dressage modelled on the classic school of Vienna. They were followed by two other girls, scantily dressed, who did acrobatics, leaping and somersaulting on the bare backs of their horses. After that came a horse race, in which four more beautiful girls, dressed like jockeys, urged their mounts round five laps of the arena, encouraged by the cheers of their gentlemen admirers. Next came one of the specialities of the Cirque Alfredi, a chariot race. Five chariots, each drawn by four horses and driven by yet more beautiful girls, raced in a reconstruction of the epic events of ancient Rome. The race roused the spectators to a frenzy of excitement. Two of the chariots collided and their drivers, wearing brief imitations of a Roman toga, were carried off on stretchers; a third overturned, throwing its driver to the ground, and in the end only a few centimetres separated the remaining two chariots as they crossed the finishing line.

The final event of the evening was the great spectacle of the circus, the military parade, headed by the master of ceremonies, who had changed his top hat, tail coat and white breeches for a splendid uniform of scarlet decorated with gold and silver braid. He was followed by a squadron of girls dressed as hussars and mounted on black horses, a band resplendent in a uniform reminiscent of the Swiss guards, four elephants drawing gun carriages, eight camels ridden by girls in the uniform of the camel corps but with their faces blackened, more hussars, Jeanne d'Arc in golden armour on a white horse, foot soldiers and finally a state carriage from which an actor in a cocked hat gave a passable imitation of Napoleon as he bowed to the crowd on each side of the arena.

When the parade had left the arena and the last echoes of applause had died away, the Duchesse de Paiva turned to Gautier and said: "My other guests have all accepted an invitation to come to my home now for supper. You will join us, I hope."

"Only if it does not inconvenience you, Madame."

"On the contrary, if you were not to come we ladies would outnumber the men excessively."

They drove back to the duchesse's house in two of the four coaches that she was reputed to own, Gautier and Juliette riding in one with the duchesse herself and the Comte de Menilmont, while the rest of the party followed in a slightly less luxuriously fitted brougham. The duchesse was in excellent spirits, as though visiting the circus had rekindled happy memories of the days when she was admired and desired by the princes, dukes and ambassadors who went to the Hippodrome to see her.

"I do wish Marie-Thérèse could have been with us tonight," she said to the others as they were driving to her home. "She would have loved that display of riding."

"Were you expecting her to be with us?" Juliette asked.

"Yes, but unfortunately she had to change her plans at the last minute."

"You and I must sympathize with each other, Madame, for we have both been disappointed." There was no rancour in the Comte de Menilmont's remark and he laughed ruefully as he made it.

"Everyone knows that young girls unaccountably change their minds," the duchesse said. "Constancy is not a virtue valued very highly by the young. But then, sometimes they have second thoughts and change their minds again."

"Ah, if only I might believe that could happen!"

Gautier was surprised at the apparent tactlessness of the duchesse in mentioning the name of Marie-Thérèse in front of the comte and even more surprised at the comte's good humour. One would not have expected a man who valued his breeding and his ancestry so highly and whose pride was always bordering on arrogance, to have accepted a rebuff from the daughter of a bourgeois parvenu so gracefully.

Feeling that it might be wise to change the subject of conversation he remarked to the duchesse: "I see you are not wearing your necklace today, Madame."

"No, the clasp still has not been repaired."

"Have you ever thought of having a copy made to wear on public occasions, as I understand some ladies do?"

"Yes, but I would get no pleasure from wearing a cheap imitation."

Her ready reply showed that the duchesse had doubtless been asked the same question many times before, but although in the darkness he could not see her expression he saw her head turn quickly as she looked at him. He suspected that she had somehow guessed he now knew that the necklace was only a copy and that she had sold the original.

They arrived at her home in Avenue des Champs Elysées. Although it was not more than twenty years old, the house had been constructed in a curious medley of architectural styles, baroque, rococo and even Gothic. When he had decided to build himself a house in Paris, the Duc de Paiva had followed the fashion set by several wealthy men. His mansion did not compare in extravagance with the pink marble palace of Comte Boni de Castellane in Avenue du Bois but it was as large if not larger than the home which the owner of the Louvre department store, Chauchard, had built for his mistress Marie Boursin and as grandiose as the strange Renaissance palace of Eugène Gaillard in Place Malesherbes, in which people said one had to wear medieval costume to feel at ease.

The supper was served in the smaller of the two drawing-rooms, which was still large enough to seat sixteen people and was panelled in dark oak and lit by electric lamps, which many people still considered an unacceptable innovation since electricity was so unflattering to a woman's complexion. They ate quails' eggs, cold duckling in aspic, fresh asparagus and a sorbet with Grand Marnier and for wine were offered Chablis and Château d'Yquem.

As they were eating, the Comte de Menilmont remarked to the duchesse: "I see that *Le Monde* published a poem by Daniele Pontana this morning. Have you met him yet?"

"Yes, once but only briefly."

"What a pity you were not at Madame Trocville's soirée on Tuesday," Madame Borde said thoughtlessly.

"I would have liked to come," the duchesse said with a comic air of regret, "but, alas, I did not have a dress to wear."

When the laughter provoked by her witticism had subsided, the comte remarked: "He really is a most gifted fellow. The poem he read at Madame Trocville's was a little masterpiece and his impersonation of the great Sarah was brilliant."

"You are right," Madame Borde agreed. "He could earn a handsome living in the theatre."

"One wonders how he does make a living," the Portuguese Vieira said. "I am told he came to France to escape his creditors."

"He lives very simply," Borde replied, "in a very modest apartment with only one servant coming in during the day."

"I have never visited him," de Menilmont said, "but they tell me he has a fine collection of arms there, including a priceless set of Italian daggers."

"Surely the apartment cannot be so small that it doesn't have at least one maid's room?" Juliette asked.

"Oh, his secretary sleeps in the maid's room," Madame Borde replied.

"I understood his secretary lived in a nearby hotel."

Madame Borde laughed. "They tell everybody that because Signor Ponzi would feel humiliated if people knew the truth. But he does sleep in the maid's room, I can assure you. My husband has visited the apartment."

"Poor man!" the duchesse exclaimed.

"It will do him no harm," Juliette commented acidly, "to experience the conditions in which women servants have to live."

Gautier had noticed during the evening that Juliette had played little part in the general conversation, only speaking when she was asked a question or when some remark was made about a subject about which she felt strongly, provoking her into a comment or a contradiction. He wondered whether she was always like that, reserved and aloof, or whether she was in a discontented mood, still brooding over what she believed was an injustice she had suffered in the matter of the Prix Fémina.

His speculations were interrupted when the Comte de Menilmont asked him: "Do you know yet who killed Abbé Didier, Inspector?"

"Not yet. But we are making progress in our enquiries."

"In our country it would be unthinkable that anyone should kill a priest," Vieira remarked. "Every man's hand would be against him. The people would seek him out and bring him to justice."

"The further south you go, the nearer you come to God," his wife added.

"Starving peasants in the south of Spain and Italy must look to God for their comfort," Juliette observed, "for they will never find it here on earth."

"I understand there is to be a requiem mass for the abbé tomorrow," Madame Borde said. The life of peasants however pitiable was not nearly so important to her as the social calendar in Paris.

"So I believe."

"Will you be going, Madame?" Gautier asked the duchesse.

"I don't think so. Why, would you expect me to?" She looked at Gautier and he thought he could detect a challenge in her stare.

"So many rich and influential people go to his church."

"Yes, but I was not one of his parishioners. In fact I have never set foot in Saint Clothilde."

Juliette and Gautier drove home at the duchesse's suggestion in one of her carriages. When they were leaving the house, Gautier told the coachman to drive first to Rue Jacob, but Juliette protested.

"You are not obliged to make any outmoded gestures of masculine chivalry for my sake," she said. "The coachman can leave you at your home first."

"I think it would be more convenient to go to Rue Jacob first."

"Where do you live?"

He told her and since they could not agree on which would be the best route, they left the coachman to decide. He took them through

Place de la Concorde, along the Seine and across Pont du Carrousel towards Rue Jacob.

"Do you live alone?" Juliette asked Gautier.

"Yes."

"But you are married?"

"In the eyes of the Church yes, but my wife left me and is living with another man."

"You don't seem unduly concerned."

"Should I be?"

"Being made a cuckold is supposed to be the greatest humiliation a man can suffer."

Gautier could remember only too vividly the misery on Suzanne's face when she had told him there was another man in her life. He said to Juliette: "Of one thing I am certain. My wife had no wish to wound me."

"You were not angry or offended?"

"What upset me was seeing the unhappiness which her feelings of guilt caused her. And I knew I must have been equally to blame."

"Do you miss her?"

"In some ways."

"Still, a man can always find consolation in other women." Gautier made no comment so she continued: "There have been other women, I suppose."

"Yes." He felt he should be resenting her

direct and personal questions, but for some reason they did not trouble him.

They were sitting side by side in the coach and as it lurched in swinging round a corner, she was thrown against him. Gautier felt the warmth of her body and the pressure of her hip and thigh against his own. It seemed to him that she stayed leaning against him rather longer than she need have done, but he dismissed the idea as absurd. On the occasions when they had been together, Juliette had shown no interest whatsoever in him as a man and her attitude towards him had been one of indifference, punctuated with spurts of antagonism or curiosity.

"What kind of women do you take to your bed?" she asked unexpectedly.

He laughed and replied flippantly: "Those that attract me."

"It's easy for a man. He can keep a mistress, visit a bordello, make love to another man's wife and no one will raise an eyebrow. In fact it's expected of him. Men who have no affairs are either despised or suspected by other men. But a woman who behaved in the same way would be ostracized."

"Society is becoming more liberal. Attitudes are changing."

"Do you have no scruples about making love to a woman, as long as you find her attractive?"

Her questions and the clinical manner in which she asked them should have irritated him. Coming from another woman he would certainly have resented them. All he said to Juliette was: "You ask almost as many questions as a policeman."

The coach was travelling along a narrow street and the sound of the horses' hooves on the cobblestones reverberated, bouncing from one side to the other off the tall, gloomy buildings. A tipsy man stumbled into the middle of the street, forcing the horses to swerve and one of them neighed in fright. The coachman cursed the man who replied with an old Parisian obscenity.

When the coach came to a halt outside her house, Juliette laid one hand on Gautier's arm. "Would you like to come in for a while?" she asked. "It isn't very late."

"What about the duchesse's coachman?"

"Oh, let him go. There are always fiacres on the corner."

"All right then. Thank you."

His first impulse had been to refuse her invitation but habit was too strong. Since Suzanne had left him, conscious that only an empty apartment awaited him he had gradually allowed himself to begin finding excuses for delaying his return home, for prolonging each evening.

They dismissed the coachman and she let the two of them into her house, unlocking the front door with a key she was carrying. Gautier wondered whether her consideration for others and her compassion for working people would not allow her to keep servants up late at night as most employers would do, waiting for her return. She showed him into her study and then went to make them a grog, returning presently with a jug of hot water, a decanter of brandy, a bowl of sugar and two glasses on a silver tray. As he mixed the drinks, she explained that she liked her grogs made with brandy because she detested the smell of rum.

"I'm sorry I was short-tempered with you at the circus," she said as they were sitting with their drinks.

"It doesn't matter."

"I thought you were suggesting that the

185

friendship between Jeanne and Marie-Thérèse was unnatural."

"What on earth do you mean?"

"The gossips of Paris are now trying to make out that Jeanne has lesbian inclinations. It has become the fashionable slander of our time. Every beautiful or successful woman is branded as a lesbian; even those who make their livelihood by sleeping with men—Caroline Otero, Liane de Pougy, Emilienne d'Alençon—they are all supposed to find secret solace in affairs with other women. We can blame that miserable little literary hack, Taxil, for this."

Léo Taxil was a writer who in the 1890s had specialized in books which purported to uncover sensational facts about the Church, freemasonry and society. In one of them, *La Corruption Fin de Siècle*, he had "exposed" the depraved immorality to be found among the wealthy and had given graphic descriptions of a growing cult of lesbian love among society ladies, of their secret meeting places and of the ways in which they recognized each other.

"I'm not a lesbian," Juliette said.

Gautier looked at her, uncertain of whether her remark was supposed to be a statement or a challenge, of whether she was being defensive or defiant. He said: "I never supposed you were."

"Many people do."

"Isn't that because you encourage them in the idea by wearing men's clothes and imitating men's behaviour?"

"I do that for another completely different reason."

"Yes, I realize that, but other people might not."

She stared moodily into her empty glass. Suddenly she seemed to lose patience, much as a governess loses patience with a singularly obtuse or stubborn child. Reaching out, she set her glass down decisively on the table beside her.

"It is growing late," she told Gautier. "You had better leave."

"Of course."

She accompanied him from the study into the hallway of the house where he collected his hat and coat and from there to the front door. After opening the door for him, she hesitated.

"I suppose you know my real reason for inviting you here tonight," she said suddenly.

"No. Should I?"

"I intended to seduce you."

He looked at her incredulously. "You cannot be serious."

She ignored his remark. "It would seem that I cannot even manage that elementary feminine function."

In the darkness of the hall Gautier could not make out the expression on her face. He felt his resolution being tugged by conflicting urges. Part of him, aware that she was an attractive and desirable woman, was tempted to probe her remark further and to discover whether she was really offering what she seemed to be; another part recoiled, unwilling to start the pretence of affection which casual sex demanded and reluctant to begin what might be an emotional attachment with a woman he felt he did not wholly understand.

"If you really had wanted to," he said, sheltering behind a defence of flippancy, "you would know how."

12

"DIES IRAE, DIES ILLA, solvet saeclum in favilla . . ." Standing at the back of the congregation in the church of Sainte Clothilde next morning, Gautier heard the priest intoning the first of the nineteen verses of the Dies Irae, part of the mass for the dead. He had arrived just as the mass for Abbé Didier was about to start and had found the church full to overflowing, every chair taken and people standing along both sides of the nave and at the back. In addition to the wealthy parishioners from the Faubourg who were sitting mainly in the front of the congregation, a great throng of ordinary people had found time to come and hear the mass.

Three priests were officiating, each wearing a black cope and black stole over his white surplice. With their slow funereal movements, they seemed to Gautier like chessmen, part of a mournful game that was being played out while the long white candles on the altar stood guard. The congregation was the audience;

ladies from the Faubourg with black veils that hid their thoughts and feelings; working women with black shawls over their heads, many of whom were weeping silently.

The celebrant intoned the Tract: "Absolve, O Lord, the souls of all the faithful departed from every bond of sin. And by the help of Your Grace may they be enabled to escape the avenging judgement."

Wrath, revenge, judgement, Gautier reflected, was what the Church warned men to expect from a supernatural power after death. On earth it was mere men like himself who were supposed to be the instrument of man's revenge. He found himself wondering whether the person who had killed Abbé Didier would ever be found and brought to judgement. He wondered too whether the killer was even now among the congregation, listening to the prayers for the dead priest's soul.

Finally the mass was over and the priest dismissed the congregation not with the usual "Ite missa est", but with a final reference to the departed soul: "Requiescat in pace".

The people drifted out of the church, some stopping in the porch and on the steps to talk, others leaving at once for their homes or their work. In the streets that bordered the small square in front of the church, several coaches stood in line waiting for their owners. Among them Gautier recognized the unmistakably opulent equipage of the Duchesse de Paiva. Walking over towards it, he took up a position near the carriage and waited. When the duchesse came out of the church she was with Monsieur and Madame de Saules and their daughter. Like the duchesse, Madame de Saules was wearing a black veil but Marie-Thérèse's face was uncovered. Gautier wondered whether this was because she was only a girl of eighteen or whether it was a gesture of protest, a sign of the resentment she had felt towards Abbé Didier for trying to interfere in her life.

The duchesse stayed talking with the banker and his family on the steps of the church for several minutes. When finally she came towards her coach, she recognized Gautier and beckoned to him.

"As you see, I did come to the requiem mass after all, Inspector."

"So I see."

"Monsieur and Madame de Saules asked me particularly if I would be present." She looked at Gautier. "And you? Why are you here?"

"I too was invited; by the curate Father Xavier."

"I thought you might have come to speak with me."

Gautier might have pointed out that she had told him she would not be going to the requiem mass. Instead he asked her: "What makes you think that?"

"You know about my necklace, don't you?" Even though there was no one within earshot, she lowered her voice, subconsciously, to protect her secret.

"I know the one you were wearing at the Tir aux Pigeons was a copy, yes."

"How did you find out?"

"The thief who tried to steal it told me. Evidently he's something of an expert on jewels."

His answer, even though it was only part of the truth, seemed to satisfy the duchesse. She said: "I must explain my reasons for having a copy made."

"You are not obliged to, Madame. It is entirely your affair."

"No, I must tell you everything. I want you to understand, Inspector."

"In that case I am, of course, at your disposal."

"Not now and not here." She reached out and laid a hand on his arm persuasively. "We'll talk later and in private. Can you come to my home this afternoon? Shall we say at five o'clock?"

Gautier bowed slightly. "I shall be there, Madame."

The coachman was already sitting on his box and at a sign from the duchesse he shook his reins and the horses ambled away. Gautier turned and began to cross the square in front of the church towards Rue St. Dominique. For a reason which he would not have been able to explain, he felt a sudden quickening of interest, a sense of anticipation, aroused by the rendezvous he had just made. Commonsense told him that the duchesse would not be inviting him to her home unless the matter which she wished to discuss with him was important, but instinct suggested she was not to be trusted too readily. She had lied to him once already.

He had crossed the square and was turning into Rue St. Dominique when he heard his name called out. A man in a light brown frock-coat, who had been following him, came up alongside. It was Daniele Pontana.

"Gautier, I must speak with you." The words were not a request, nor even a command, but more of a challenge, it seemed to Gautier.

In addition to the brown suit and a brown hat, Pontana was wearing a green embroidered waistcoat, a pale green shirt, a yellow cravat and yellow spats. Black was the prescribed colour for a man's suit, although a few eccentrics drew attention to themselves by wearing grey. An outfit in brown, green and yellow would be unthinkable at any time and scandalous for a funeral and Gautier wondered whether Pontana, like Marie-Thérèse de Saules, was defying convention as a form of protest.

"How dare you have the effrontery to question my secretary in my absence?" Pontana demanded angrily. "I have not come to France to be insulted and harassed by the police."

"I went to your apartment to speak with you, Monsieur. As you were out, your secretary kindly agreed to answer my questions."

"You invaded my home! The Italian ambassador shall be informed of this!" Pontana was at least fifteen centimetres shorter than

Gautier which made his display of indignant rage less impressive than he probably believed.

People coming from the church were passing and several of them, hearing Pontana's strident, angry tone, looked curiously at the two men. Gautier suggested: "Wouldn't it be better if we discussed this matter elsewhere?"

"I wish to settle it now."

"All right. I am heading for Boulevard St. Germain. If you would be kind enough to accompany me for part of the way, we could talk as we walked along."

"Very well."

The worst of the Italian's temper appeared to be subsiding. Gautier was going to the Café Corneille and a disagreeable thought that Pontana might choose to accompany him all the way to the café began to depress him. He had no wish to be seen arriving at the Corneille with this scented dandy. The habitués of the café had a sophisticated but merciless wit which they had no hesitation in exercising on each other.

"By what right are you asking questions about me?" Pontana demanded as they were walking along Rue St. Dominique.

"By my authority as an officer of the Sûreté."

"Then you are misusing that authority. What I wish to know is who is employing you."

"Employing me?"

"Yes. You cannot possibly pretend that you came to my home on legitimate police business."

"Certainly I did."

"I refuse to believe you. Someone is paying you. As in Italy the police here are mere lackeys of the wealthy."

Gautier began to grow annoyed. "Monsieur, you evidently do not appreciate the seriousness of the enquiries that I am conducting. They concern the death of a priest, the Abbé Didier."

"That's only an excuse for prying into my private life. No one can believe for one moment that I am implicated in the death of that meddling priest. Admit it, you do not really believe that I killed him."

"As yet I have formed no opinion one way or the other. All I know is that you quarrelled and shouted abuse at the abbé."

Pontana smiled with the self-assurance of one whose opinions are always being proved right. "So! He told people about that. I always said that the Church cares nothing for the secrecy of the confessional."

"The abbé told no one. You were overheard when you shouted at him in the sacristy by another priest who was passing at the time."

Gautier began to feel restive. He knew it was not much more than twenty minutes' walk to the Café Corneille. Moreover he had noticed that Pontana had tried to disguise his sallow complexion with a little powder and rouge.

"I suppose you have no objection, Monsieur," he said, deciding that a direct question might bring their discussion to a head, "to telling me where you were at seven o'clock on Tuesday morning?"

Pontana looked at him and grinned cynically. "Very clever! A neat attempt to find out where I have been in the early mornings! But I shall tell you nothing."

"In that case it may be necessary to arrange for you to be brought before a juge d'instruction." Gautier knew that the threat was a flimsy one, for no examining magistrate had yet been appointed for the case.

Pontana stopped walking and faced him. "Come, Inspector, let us not waste any more time on this charade. In any case, you have no more reason for hounding me. As you will soon find out, it's too late." He turned and strode away, decisively, like a man glad to have disposed of a piece of irritating business.

Duthrey was sitting at their usual table at the Café Corneille with the elderly lawyer, Vence of *Gil Blas* and a bookseller named Froissart who had been a regular at the café for more years than he or anyone else could remember. Besides managing his bookshop, Froissart was a patron of avant-garde poets, publishing their poems, lending them money and trying to persuade critics to recognize their talent.

When Gautier had joined them and ordered his aperitif, Duthrey remarked: "The social whirlpool which carries you around, old friend, does not appear to be abating."

"What are you talking about?"

"It is said you were at the Alfredi circus last night in the private box of the Duchesse de Paiva."

"Mother of God! Don't tell me *Figaro* has a reporter covering the circus every night!"

"Two," Duthrey replied, improvising flippantly. "One represents the gossip columns to see which members of the Jockey Club are chasing the lady riders and one is from the news page in case a wire-walker falls and breaks his neck."

"I believe you're jealous," Gautier said.

"If he is not then I am." The elderly lawyer joined in. "The Duchesse de Paiva, now there's a woman for you!"

"She's no longer available."

"Possibly not, but her eyes have not lost their fire, I can tell you."

"You should not be thinking of sex at your age," the bookseller Froissart reproached the lawyer.

"At my age what more can I do except to think about it?"

"You could improve your mind by reading poetry. I shall shortly be publishing a new review in which the best work of contemporary poets will appear. Why not take out a subscription?"

"Contemporary poets!" the lawyer exclaimed. "There hasn't been a poet in France worth reading since Victor Hugo."

"That's unfair!" Duthrey protested. "What about Verlaine, Mallarmé, Valéry?"

They began discussing French poetry, arguing over the merits of the poets of the last twenty years. In the main it was an argument between the elderly lawyer who was convinced that poetry had died with the Romantics, and Froissart, who as a young man had been an apostle of the Symbolists and who encouraged with his patronage every new movement or trend in the poetry of the day. Duthrey was inclined to side with the lawyer while Vence supported Froissart. Gautier could see some merit in the views put forward by both sides.

"We must not forget our poetesses," Froissart said. "Some of them have great talent. Anna de Noailles, for example, and Lucie Delarue Mardrus and Renée de Saules."

"Madame de Saules has been in a poetic limbo for the past fifteen years," Duthrey commented.

"She is writing again and well. Some of the verses in her latest volume are exquisite."

"It has taken her a long time to recover from the collapse of her love affair with Paul Monceau."

"Perhaps she has found consolation elsewhere," Vence suggested.

"At her age that isn't very likely."

"Well, I can think of no other reason why she should be slipping out of her house at seven o'clock in the morning and jumping into a fiacre."

"You saw her doing that?"

"Yes. A few mornings ago."

"And where, may one ask, were you going at that hour of the morning?"

"He was going home, of course."

They all laughed. Vence had the reputation of being something of a roué and his friends often teased him with accusations of spending his nights at the Chabanais or some other high class maison de tolérance. They would also invent names and descriptions for the several mistresses whom they liked to imagine he was keeping.

"When is the first number of your new review to appear?" Duthrey asked Froissart.

"In September."

"Will it include any poems by Daniele Pontana?" Gautier enquired.

"No. I could not afford the payment he would demand."

"The creature's an upstart," Duthrey remarked. "He values himself and his poetry altogether too highly."

"I feel sorry for him," Froissart replied. "He has been hounded out of his native Italy."

"Surely that was his own fault. Is he not very heavily in debt?"

"One expects poets to be in debt. But once Pontana's wife died, her father, the Duca di Ligorno, treated him shamefully. He had always hated Pontana."

"In that case why did he allow him to marry his daughter?"

"It's a long story," Froissart replied, "and for Pontana not a very creditable one."

He told them the story. As a young man from a middle class family in a small provincial town, Pontana had come to Venice determined to win for himself both a reputation as poet and a place in Venetian society. His youth, his charm and the lyrical freshness of his first volume of verses had quickly conquered the literary critics. The ladies were captivated even more easily. What woman could resist an eighteen-year-old poet with burning eyes, a head of curls and a ready compliment?

The Duchessa di Ligorno, one of the ladies who had fallen under his spell, had, rashly as it proved, invited the little provincial nobody to her house where he met her daughter Francesca. With the help of a servant, Pontana had arranged secret meetings with the girl who became so infatuated with him that she agreed they should elope. They fled by train to Verona where the police, alerted by the girl's family, intercepted them at the railway station and took them back to Venice. Faced with the terrible scandal that ensued, the Duca di Ligorno had no alternative but to allow the lovers to marry, but he took his revenge for the shame they had brought on his house by giving his daughter no dowry.

"In less than a year Pontana grew bored with his wife," Froissart said. "She had after all brought him none of the things he wanted, neither riches nor social position. Soon he was rushing from one mistress to another, all of them rich and able to gratify his extravagant tastes."

"And his wife put up with this behaviour?" Duthrey asked.

"She did. They say she was a saint. But once she was dead the scene changed. I was in Venice a few weeks ago and I can tell you Pontana's life had been made intolerable."

"How did she die, anyway?"

"She fell from a window of their house and was killed. No one knows how it happened. Officially her death has been recorded as an accident, but Pontana was alone with her in the room at the time."

"So people began suggesting he pushed her to her death."

"Precisely."

Before leaving the Sûreté that morning for the requiem mass, Gautier had told Surat to make certain enquiries in the vicinity of Pontana's apartment in Rue du Cherche-Midi. He wanted to know anything that could be learnt about the movements of Pontana and Ponzi over the last few days and of any visitors they might have had. In particular he wished to know whether any women had visited the apartment and if so at what time they had arrived and left. When he returned to headquarters after lunching, he saw that Surat had completed the assignment and his report was lying on Gautier's desk.

Confidential Report

For Inspector J-P. Gautier
Acting on your instructions I visited Rue du Cherche-Midi and made enquiries about the establishment of Signor Pontana. I learnt that the one servant he employs, an elderly woman, arrives at the apartment at nine

o'clock each morning when she cleans the house and if required prepares a meal at mid-day. I decided it would be imprudent to speak to her and talked instead with a girl who works in the baker's shop below the apartment and to the proprietor of a café just along the street. The girl, who is evidently dazzled by Pontana's reputation as a lady-killer, knew a surprising amount about his movements and the café owner, since business at his establishment is very slack, had little to do except to stand at his doorway and watch the world. Both the baker's shop and the café open each morning at 6 o'clock.

From the two sources I established that women frequently visit the apartment during both the day and night. It would seem that Pontana has a voracious appetite for sex and on several occasions has been known to take women back to his home who, from their manner of dress, can only have been those who frequent café-concerts and music halls. Women have been seen leaving his house early in the morning. There are no reports that he has ever been visited by a lady of quality.

As to the movements of the two men, the

secretary Ponzi seldom leaves the apartment except on short business errands or to take a mid-day aperitif. Pontana usually goes out every day to lunch and in the evening, often returning late. Once or twice he has been seen leaving home early in the morning dressed in riding attire and on these occasions he returned home about two hours later.

When he had finished reading the report, Gautier sent for Surat and explained a plan of action which was to be put into effect immediately. Surat was to select two reliable men and send them to Rue du Cherche-Midi, where they were to keep watch on Pontana's apartment.

"And what are they to be watching for?" Surat asked.

"They must make a note of everyone who either enters or leaves the apartment, but what I particularly want to know is Pontana's movements. If he leaves his apartment then one of the men should follow him while the other returns here at once to tell us."

"You don't want me to be there with them?"

"No," Gautier replied. "I have another task for you. Do you have contacts in the SNCF?"

"The railways? Yes, as a matter of fact I

have. My wife's cousin is married to a man who works in the head office."

"Then he's just the man we need."

He asked Surat to find out whether reservations had been made in the name of Pontana on any of the main international express trains leaving Paris that evening. Surat's relative should make immediate enquiries to this effect, starting with trains that might be leaving the Gare du Nord for Belgium or England.

"Do you believe the Italian will be attempting to leave Paris?" Surat asked.

"It's only a guess. But Pontana is a gambler and gamblers who have made one successful coup often cannot resist trying it again."

13

THE Duchesse de Paiva received Gautier that evening in a room on the first floor of her home which was decorated in a style quite unlike that of the remainder of the house. The carpets and curtains were of a bold design, almost startlingly so, and the furniture painted in bright colours. On one wall hung three framed posters advertising some of the circuses in which Jeanne Baroche had appeared, the Hippodrome, the Cirque d'Eté and the exclusive Cirque Molier. One of the posters was a caricature of Jeanne herself, then the circus's leading rider, beautifully executed in a few simple lines. Elsewhere in the room were mementoes of the circus and of her career; a scarlet riding whip, a framed letter from the Minister of the Interior thanking Jeanne Baroche for appearing in a charity fête in the Parc Bagatelle, a miniature pair of spurs in gold set with rubies, a signed photograph of the famous clowns Footit and Chocolat, a head-dress of ostrich feathers.

Gautier guessed that the room was the duchesse's own creation, part boudoir, part private drawing-room, a room to which she invited her intimate friends. No doubt, however, it was not the room in which she entertained Monsieur de Saules.

She was wearing a loosely fitting green silk dress with puff sleeves and had allowed her black hair to fall down over her shoulders. It was the first time Gautier had seen her with her hair down and he wondered whether this gesture of informality was supposed to have a significance. She was reclining on a chaise-longue and made him draw up a chair to sit near her.

"So you know my secret?" She smiled as she asked the question.

"I know the necklace you showed me was a copy."

"Is that all you know?"

"Is there more?"

"Come, Monsieur Gautier." She had been fanning herself with an exquisite painted Japanese fan. Now she folded it and tapped Gautier's arms with it in playful reproach. "You are not being quite honest with me. Admit it, you have discovered somehow that I have sold the original necklace."

"I have heard a rumour to that effect."

"In that case I must tell you why I sold it."

"You are not obliged to."

"I know, but I wish to nevertheless. You see, I am going to ask you a very great favour. I am going to ask you to keep what you know to yourself and it is only fair that I should explain why."

"As you wish."

"The person who bought the necklace from me gave me half a million francs, which is perhaps one half of its true value, but I needed the money." She paused and looked at Gautier as though to make sure she had his attention for what she was next going to say. "Not for me, but for my daughter."

"I did not know you had a daughter."

"Very few people do, so please, Monsieur Gautier, treat what I am going to tell you in confidence."

The father of her daughter, the duchesse told him, was a Belgian, a prince of royal blood, whom she had met many years previously when she had been starting her career in the circus. When he knew she was going to have a child, the prince wished to marry her in spite of the opposition of the Belgian court, but knowing what a sacrifice marriage would have meant for him, she had refused. So she had given birth to the daughter secretly and sent the baby to the country where it had been brought up by a good, pious middle-class family. Now the girl was seventeen and so beautiful that she had captured the love of the youngest son of an aristocratic family who lived in a nearby château.

"They wish to be married," the duchesse said, "and the boy's family have given their consent, but she must have a dowry, a dowry worthy of the marriage."

The duchesse was a good story-teller, embellishing her narrative with inventive phrases and picturesque descriptions and as he listened, Gautier found himself wondering why the tale she was telling sounded familiar. When she had finished, he remarked: "Was there no other way you could find the money?"

"You ask that because I live in this vast house with its beautiful furniture and because I have servants and carriages and expensive clothes." She smiled sadly. "None of it is mine."

"I assumed it was your inheritance from your late husband."

"Many people believe that but it isn't true. Everything belongs to the duc's children by his first marriage. I have the use of the house during my lifetime and an income to run it and clothe myself but nothing more. I can sell nothing, not even a single picture."

"In that case, Madame, by selling the necklace you are making a very great sacrifice."

"What mother would not sell a necklace for her daughter's happiness?"

Gautier nodded to show he accepted the point. He knew that the duchesse would be expecting him to make some comment, to give some sign that he understood and sympathized with the story she had told him, but the mood of scepticism and mistrust which he had felt when he had arrived at her house had still not dissipated.

"I sold the necklace willingly," she continued, "but I would rather the person who gave it to me did not know."

"Would that be Monsieur de Saules?"

"You're a clever man," she said and sighed. "Yes, it was he who gave the necklace to me

212

and you can understand why he must not find out that I have sold it."

"He doesn't know you have a daughter?"

"My God, no!"

The duchesse had been reclining in the chaise-longue with her legs up, looking decorative and at ease. It was a pose often favoured by ladies of the demi-monde in studio photographs or portraits. Now she sat up, turning in the chair and leaning forward. The décolletage of her dress would have been thought daring in an evening gown and her purpose in wearing it at that time of day could only have been to show she was still a seductive and desirable woman.

"You see how I have put myself completely in your hands by telling you my secrets," she said, laying a hand on Gautier's arm. "Can I rely on your discretion?"

"If what you have told me is the truth, I will certainly not repeat it."

"That means you don't believe me!"

"It means I reserve my judgement."

"Your mistrust of me is quite unjustified," she complained.

"Not at all. By your own admission, you did not tell me the truth before."

"About the necklace, I agree, but I have explained my reasons for that."

"You lied to me in another matter as well."

"What matter?"

"You told me you did not know Abbé Didier and had never been to his church, when the truth is that you went to see him in the sacristy of his church only a few days ago."

For a brief moment panic flared in her eyes. Her mind, like a bird trapped in a room, seemed to be darting everywhere looking for an escape in denials, bluster, another lie. Then she recovered her composure. She said slowly: "Yes. I did not tell you the truth about that, but for the same reason."

"The same reason?"

"It was the church which helped look after my daughter. Years ago when the abbé was just a priest, he found her the home in the country. From time to time he used to visit the family and it was he who took the money from me for her dowry and helped arrange the marriage."

"Did you give him the money in gold?"

"Of course!" She looked at him sharply. "Why do you ask?"

"If he had such a large sum in his keeping, it might well have been a reason for his murder."

"Well it wasn't. I happen to know that the money reached the family who are looking after my daughter."

Taking out his pocket-watch, Gautier saw that it was almost six-thirty. The Duchesse de Paiva had kept him waiting for a full twenty minutes when he had arrived and they had been talking for an hour. It was time that he was returning to the Sûreté to hear whether the men whom Surat had posted outside Pontana's apartment had anything to report.

"Thank you, Madame, for being so frank with me," he told the duchesse.

"Could you not call me by my Christian name? Formality only makes me feel uncomfortable."

He bowed slightly. "If you wish."

"And may I ask what your name is?"

"Jean-Paul."

He rose from his chair and she put out a hand to restrain him. "Surely you don't have to leave so soon?"

"Unfortunately yes. I still have work to do."

"Let it wait until tomorrow. We can have a little dinner here together, just the two of us."

"It's very kind of you, but I must leave."

The duchesse stood up and faced him. She

smiled and he was aware, as she meant him to be, of the sensual warmth and appeal of her body. She said very softly: "It is such a long time since I spent the evening with a young, virile man."

At another time and in different circumstances, Gautier would have been tempted by the invitation and the challenge it implied. Instead he felt a distaste not at her blatancy but at her disloyalty. He felt certain from what he knew of Armand de Saules that the banker must be a considerate, generous and constant lover.

He bent over the duchesse's hand as he raised it to his lips. "You could easily find a score of men more worthy than I, who would fight for the honour."

When he arrived back at Quai des Orfévres, Gautier met Surat coming out of Sûreté headquarters. Surat said: "I was coming to fetch you, Patron. Pontana left his apartment half an hour ago with two valises."

"Do we know where he was headed?"

"Not yet. His fiacre made for the Seine, crossed it and then turned towards Rue de Rivoli. Our two men followed it together for a time and then one of them came back here to report. The other will be in touch with us in due course. But I also have news from my wife's cousin."

"Excellent! What has he found out?"

"That two reservations have been made in the name of Pontana for the wagon-lit on the night express which leaves the Gare de Lyon for Milan."

"Milan! I never expected he would go back to Italy."

"That's the reason why we have only just heard from my wife's cousin. He checked all the night trains for other destinations first and only tried Italy as a last chance."

"What time is the train due to leave?" Gautier asked.

"At eight fifteen."

"Good! Then we have plenty of time. Let's make for the station."

"Shall we take a police wagon? I have one standing by."

"No. This isn't a case when we can treat the man like a criminal."

The fiacre in which Gautier had ridden back from his meeting with the Duchesse de Paiva was still in the street outside the Sûreté. The coachman had pulled across to the river side and was sitting on his box eating from a hunk of bread which he held in one hand and a large salami sausage which he was holding in the other. A half empty bottle of red wine stood on the seat beside him.

Crossing to the fiacre, Gautier and Surat asked the man to take them to the Gare de Lyon. With an ill grace he agreed to do so, but only after he had finished his meal. Everyone had a right to eat he grumbled, and it was impossible to say when he would next be able to sit down to a proper meal.

"Did the men who were watching Pontana's apartment have anything else to report?" Gautier asked Surat when at last they finally moved off.

"Nothing."

"No one called at the place?"

"No. They had no visitors."

The journey to the station took only a few minutes. Although no doubt the grand boulevards would be crowded with people who were starting off on an evening of gaiety, the rest of the city was unusually quiet, as though subdued by the lethargy which follows a hot and tiring day. The worst of the July day's heat had passed but the evening was heavy and airless.

The leaves hung listlessly from the trees which bordered the streets.

They arrived at the Gare de Lyon with a full half-hour in hand before the night express was due to leave. The man from the Sûreté was waiting for them in the forecourt.

"Have they boarded the train yet?" Gautier asked him.

"No, Inspector."

"Is there a lady with him?"

"No."

"Then what is he doing? Waiting by the platform?"

The man looked bewildered. "But he's no longer here."

"Are you saying he has left? Mother of God, why did you not follow him then?"

"He was taken away by the police."

"You must be mistaken," Surat said sharply.

"No. Inspector Lemaire and two men from the Sûreté took him away in a wagon."

14

THE activity in Sûreté headquarters at eight o'clock on a summer evening was astonishing. When Gautier and Surat reached Quai des Orfèvres, they found policemen looking alert, messengers scurrying around the corridors and an atmosphere which inexperienced visitors might have mistaken for zeal, but which cynical members of the organization would have recognized as a well-practised charade. It could only mean that the Director-General was in the building, a fact surprising in itself since Courtrand led a demanding social life which normally required him to leave his office at six every evening and not infrequently a good deal earlier. This evening, Gautier was told by the policeman on duty at the entrance to the building, the Director-General was in his room interrogating Pontana, who had been taken up there as soon as the wagon had returned from the Gare de Lyon.

Gautier took Surat up to his own office and from the drawer of his table took the telegraph message he had received the previous day from the chief of police in Venice. He read the first few words of the telegraph for a second time.

"Look. I thought at the time there was something odd about this," he said, holding the telegraph out to Surat. "The message begins with the words 'We repeat'. Now I wonder why they should have used that phrase."

"The original message was in Italian. Perhaps it's a mistranslation."

"You think that what they really meant to say was 'We declare' or 'We confirm'? I suppose that's possible."

"Have you another explanation?"

"Perhaps. Go and see if you can find out whether there had been an earlier message from Venice."

Surat went downstairs and was soon back, carrying another message form in his hand. He told Gautier: "You were right. This almost identical message was received from the chief of police in Venice only twenty-four hours before yours."

"To whom was it addressed?"

"It's a reply to a request for information about Pontana sent by the Director-General."

"As I suspected. I must go and find out what

221

he's up to. While I'm doing that get over to Pontana's apartment. If the secretary, Ponzi, is still there, bring him in for questioning."

After Surat had left, Gautier went down to the Director's office on the first floor. Evidently Courtrand must have finished his questioning of Pontana for he was alone, trying with little success to telephone. Although telephones were now becoming commonplace in Paris, the service was far from efficient and callers were dependent on the operators who were an autocratic breed, liable to disconnect anyone who in their opinion was not treating them with sufficient respect. Courtrand, never a patient man, was arguing with the operator and gradually losing his temper. Finally he put the instrument down and threw his hands in the air.

"What is the use of this mechanical contraption," he complained loudly, "if it doesn't work? Now I shall have to go and deliver my message in person."

"May I speak with you before you go, Monsieur?" Gautier asked him.

"Surely it can wait until tomorrow. My wife and I have guests for dinner and I am late already."

"It has to do with the Italian, Pontana. I am

told he was arrested this evening at the Gare de Lyon by Inspector Lemaire."

"That is so. Why do you ask?"

"Surely, Monsieur le Directeur, I am supposed to be in charge of the investigations into the death of Abbé Didier."

"What are you talking about, Gautier?" Courtrand asked impatiently. "Pontana was arrested on my instructions, for reasons which have nothing to do with the abbé's death."

"I have had Pontana kept under surveillance as a possible suspect in the Didier affair."

Courtrand made an exaggerated gesture of despair. "Not again! How often must I tell you, Gautier, that respectable, well-to-do people do not go around murdering or poisoning or stabbing."

"Pontana's wife died under suspicious circumstances and people in Italy believe he may have been responsible. On top of that we have evidence that he quarrelled with the abbé."

Courtrand thought for a while about what Gautier had told him before replying. Eventually he said grudgingly: "Well, the man is an Italian, I suppose." Courtrand's xenophobia was notorious. He hated all foreigners including the English, although he affected many English mannerisms and modelled his style of dress on that of England's king. "And if what you say is true we have good reason for holding him here at least overnight."

Taking a bunch of keys from his pocket, he began locking the drawers of his desk. Then he rose, crossed the room and checked that the small safe in which he kept confidential documents was also securely locked. This, Gautier knew, was part of the routine which the Director followed every evening before he left his office with the care of a man who revered ceremony. Next he would take his top hat down from the hat-stand, brush it on his elbow, put it on and study the effect in a mirror which he kept concealed, lying face down on a nearby cabinet. A comb would then be produced from his waistcoat pocket for a few flourishes to tidy his beard and moustaches and the Director-General would be ready to go out and face the world, with all the confidence of a man who knew and respected his position in life.

"Why was Pontana arrested then?" Gautier asked as he watched the performance.

"Because he was about to abduct a young woman."

"How do you know that? Was she with him at the station?"

"She was not there when he was arrested, but then without doubt she intended to arrive at the station only just before the train was due to leave and thus lessen the chances that they would be prevented from leaving the country."

"Did Pontana admit he was waiting for her?"

"Of course not! The man isn't stupid. He claimed he was waiting for his secretary and that the two of them intended leaving together for Milan." Courtrand had his hat on by this time and was ready to leave. He said with heavy sarcasm: "I trust that answers all your questions, Gautier."

"I have one more, Monsieur."

"What is it?"

"You have been making enquiries about Pontana with the chief of police in Venice. May I ask why?"

"It seems strange that the Director-General of the Sûreté should be questioned by one of his inspectors," Courtrand replied acidly, "but I will tell you if it makes you any happier. I was requested to make enquiries about Pontana in confidence by the mother of a young woman, a very important person, Madame de Saules. I

225

am now going to her house to tell her that her daughter is safe from the scoundrel."

Taking his walking stick from the hat-stand, he left the room with the complacent air of a man who has put a troublesome subordinate firmly in his place. Instead of returning to his own office, Gautier too went downstairs and leaving the building walked to a café around the corner in Place Dauphine. It was a small, unpretentious place owned by a mother and daughter from Normandy. The food, although never lacking in flavour, was inclined to be heavy and so were the two women, but Gautier had become friendly with them and ate his evening meal there more often than not. He was not sure why. Place Dauphine was itself attractive, a small quiet triangular space bordered by trees, and after a late evening at the Sûreté the café was a convenient place to eat and to while away time, delaying his return to an empty apartment. Sometimes Gautier wondered whether the real attraction for him might not be the daughter, Janine. She had a pleasant, good-natured face and an ample but not unattractive body and it surprised him that she had not yet married. Often when she leant over him to set a plate or a bottle of wine on the table, he felt her body brush against his shoulder and would ask himself whether, if he invited her, she would go home with him that night and if so how her body would feel lying against his own in bed.

Tonight the café was almost empty and Janine had time to chat and joke with him. After starting his meal with *andouillettes* he had a plate of *rillettes de lapin de Garenne*, a speciality from Evreux. It was Janine who suggested the *rillettes*, a dish made from wild rabbits whose prodigious fertility was the subject of rustic jokes throughout Normandy. He supposed with regret that her suggestion was not by way of being a hint, but after half a bottle of red wine and a glass of Calvados she was beginning to seem more than usually desirable.

Thoughts of sex reminded him of the Duchesse de Paiva. He had suspected at the time and was certain now that she had invited him to her house that evening and tried to keep him there until the train which Pontana had planned to take had left Paris. Had he known that Courtrand was also having the Italian watched and would have him arrested at the Gare de Lyon, he would have accepted the duchesse's invitation. The irony of what might then have happened appealed to his sense of humour.

He was still smiling at the thought when Surat came into the café. He was expecting him because he had left a message at the Sûreté saying where he was to be found.

"Well, did you find Signor Ponzi at the apartment?" he asked his assistant. "Or had he fled as well?"

"No, he was still there."

"And you brought him back with you?"

"I couldn't do that. Ponzi is dead. We found him lying on the floor of the apartment, stabbed through the heart."

Ponzi's body lay stretched out on the floor of the living-room of the apartment. The expression on the face, unlike that on the face of Abbé Didier's corpse, was one of complete peace. Perhaps to die in tranquillity, Gautier reflected, was the reward for a lifetime of devoted service, not to all men but to one man.

He could detect no signs of a struggle or a fight in the room. On the floor against one wall stood two leather suitcases, while through the open door he could see in the bedroom two large tin trunks, a wooden box, two hat-boxes and a cabin trunk of the type much favoured by travellers, which could be stood on end and opened to serve as a wardrobe during a sea voyage. The suitcases, faded and worn, were stamped with Ponzi's initials and presumably they carried all the secretary's possessions, while the trunks, boxes and hat-boxes were filled with his master's more lavish wardrobe. Gautier noticed that every item of furniture in the two rooms had been methodically labelled as though they were shortly to be collected by furniture removers. The address on the labels read "Palazzo Fabbri, Venezia". Pontana, it seemed, had been planning to return to Venice in style.

He examined Ponzi's body. The stab wound was clean and neat and very little blood had been shed. There was no sign of a weapon but the wound suggested that it had been made by a slim dagger, not unlike the one which must have been used to kill Abbé Didier. Gautier glanced across the room to where during his previous visit to the apartment he had seen a set of daggers hanging on the wall. They had been taken down and lay, still mounted on their wooden rack, on a table nearby. None of the five daggers were missing.

Ponzi's left hand was clutching an envelope which had been crumpled by a last convulsive grip as he died. Prising open the stiffened fingers, Gautier took it and smoothed it out. It was addressed in a flowing, feminine hand to Signor Enrico Ponzi and had been slit open but was now empty. Gautier looked on the floor near the body, on an armchair nearby and on a writing-desk in the room, but could find no letter that the envelope might have contained.

"Do you think Pontana killed him before he left for the Gare de Lyon?" Surat asked.

"What motive could he have for doing so?"

"If he killed the abbé, Ponzi might well have known about it."

"So Pontana killed him to make sure he told no one?"

"Why not?" Surat was beginning to be attracted by his theory. "Pontana was counting on getting away to Milan this evening. He probably assumed that in that case Ponzi's body would not be found until the furniture removers arrived here tomorrow. Then we might well have assumed that he had been killed during the night by an intruder."

Gautier could think of several reasons why Surat's hypothesis was unconvincing but he did not give any of them. Instead he said: "Ask Bastat to come in for a moment. I'd like a few words with him."

Bastat was the policeman who had followed Pontana to the Gare de Lyon. He had accompanied Gautier and Surat back to the Sûreté from the station and then come with them to Rue du Cherche-Midi. Gautier had stationed him outside the building to watch for the doctor who had been sent for to examine Ponzi's body, and to keep away any curious spectators.

When he came into the apartment, Gautier asked him: "Do you recall at what time Pontana left the apartment to go to the station?"

"Yes, Inspector, I made a note of the time. It was a few minutes after six fifteen."

"That was a long time before his train was due to leave."

"He didn't go straight to the station. I followed him in a fiacre first to Rue de Castiglione where he entered a tailor's establishment. He was there for more than half an hour and came out followed by the tailor who was carrying two suits over his arm.

Pontana had left his valises in the fiacre and the tailor packed the suits into one of them. From there he went to a hatter in Rue de la Paix and collected a hat-box. Finally he set out for the Gare de Lyon and then, as you already know, he was arrested there not long after he arrived."

"My God! He's a cool customer that one!" Surat exclaimed. "Stopping to buy new clothes when he was fleeing the country!"

Gautier smiled. "Obviously he has discovered that our tailors have a better sense of style than those in his native land."

"When I was waiting downstairs just now," Bastat said, "I found this letter lying in the street outside the building. It appears to have been written to this man, Ponzi."

Gautier took the folded sheet of notepaper which Bastat held out to him and which was of the same colour as the envelope he had found clutched in Ponzi's hand. The letter read:

Dear Signor Ponzi,

When I met Signor Pontana the other day, he told me that he was planning to write a verse drama on a theme connected with the Norse legends of the Nibelungs. He also said he was hampered in reading and understanding the background to these mythological sagas since he has no knowledge of Scandinavian languages.

This letter therefore is to introduce to you Madame Inga Ducroix. She is a lady who has fallen on hard times following the sad death of her husband who was one of France's most eminent lexicographers.

Madame Ducroix is a refined and cultured lady and she is supporting herself as best she can by translating and interpreting. Norwegian is her native tongue and she is also fluent in Swedish. It occurred to me, therefore, that Signor Pontana might be able to make use of her services.

Please accept, sir, the expression of
my most courteous sentiments,
Adèle Brifout.

Folding the letter, Gautier put it in the envelope and placed the envelope in his pocket. He told Surat: "I am going back to headquarters now. Stay here until the doctor arrives and tell him I would like a report on the cause of Ponzi's death, although of course it will only be a formality. Then after you have arranged for the

233

body to be taken to the mortuary, go home. You've been on duty too long as it is."

"Thank you, Patron."

"What about me?" Bastat asked. "Shall I come with you?"

"No. There's nothing to be done at headquarters except to write a report. Go home, but on your way stop and have a few words with the fiacre drivers you will find waiting on the corner just down the street. If they can tell you nothing, come back here tomorrow morning and try again. If necessary question all the drivers in the neighbourhood."

"What shall I ask them, Inspector?"

"Whether any of them brought a fare to the apartment or took one away between, say, seven and eight o'clock. I suspect it may have been a lady; a lady wearing a veil."

15

"IT is very good of you to come at this time of night to help us, Inspector," Monsieur de Saules said.

"Yes. We are most obliged to you," his wife added.

They had received Gautier in the principal drawing-room on the ground floor at the back of their house. When he had arrived back at the Sûreté from Pontana's apartment, he had found a message waiting for him from Courtrand with instructions that he was to go to the house of Monsieur de Saules as soon as possible. He had expected that he would find Courtrand there, but when he reached the house in Rue du Bac, the banker and his wife were alone.

"How can I be of service to you?" Gautier asked.

"Our daughter is missing," Madame de Saules replied.

"Missing?"

"No one in the house has seen her since early

afternoon and we have no idea where she might have gone."

"Could she have gone to visit friends?"

"Our servants have been making enquiries for the past two hours at every house where we thought she might be, but they have brought back no news."

"Did you try the Duchesse de Paiva? I know they are good friends."

"I telephoned the duchesse myself," Monsieur de Saules replied, "but she too has had no word from Marie-Thérèse."

"Do you suppose she might have left for Italy by another train?" Madame de Saules asked. "She may have suspected that Monsieur Courtrand might arrange for Pontana to be stopped at the station."

"Does that mean you think they intended to run off together?"

"It seems very likely."

"I don't share your view, Madame."

"Your director thought that was their plan. That's why he had Pontana arrested."

"I have information which Monsieur Courtrand has not heard. Where is he, by the way?"

"He had to leave for an important meeting."

Gautier resisted a temptation to laugh. In spite of all the bombast and bravado, Courtrand, like many lesser men, was afraid of displeasing his wife. He would not have risked being home late for dinner even to help an important banker.

"Do you know whether your daughter has taken any luggage with her?" he asked.

"Not as far as I can tell," Madame de Saules replied. "I looked through her wardrobes and none of her clothes appear to be missing, except of course what she was wearing."

"Did no one see her leave the house?"

"It seems not."

"Forgive me for asking you this, Madame, but have you quarrelled with your daughter?"

"Why on earth should they have quarrelled?" Monsieur de Saules asked.

"At Madame's request the Sûreté has been making enquiries in Italy concerning Signor Pontana. If your daughter had found that out, she might well have been upset. She gave me the impression that she resented any attempts to interfere in her life."

De Saules looked at his wife quickly and Gautier guessed he had not heard of

Courtrand's enquiries. He said: "Yes. She would have been very angry."

"I'm sure she knew nothing of my request to Monsieur Courtrand," Madame de Saules said. "And certainly we never quarrelled."

"I have one more question. Do you know whether she went riding early this morning?"

"Yes. That is she left the house to do so, but she returned home sooner than she usually did, so she may have changed her mind when she reached the Bois."

"I suspect she may have been meeting Pontana in the Bois de Boulogne during her early morning rides," Gautier said.

Madame de Saules stared at him for a moment before replying, as though she were trying to assess how much he knew. Finally she said reluctantly: "Yes, she was."

"But Renée, how do you know that?" her husband protested.

"Because I followed her one morning."

"You followed her! Secretly?" De Saules was appalled.

"It was the only way I could find out the truth. Would you have preferred me to send one of the servants to follow her or hire a detective?"

"It's shameful that you should spy on your own daughter!"

"Someone had to act," Madame de Saules replied angrily. "You let the girl do what she liked, make what friends she chose. God knows what habits she picked up from these dubious characters of the demi-monde! Yes, I found out that Marie-Thérèse was meeting this man Pontana unchaperoned and in secret in the Bois. That's why I asked Monsieur Courtrand to make enquiries in Italy. We know nothing about him or his birth or his family. People have even told me that he's married and has deserted his wife."

She was really angry. What she was saying was intended to hurt her husband and must have been her way of repaying him for humiliating her not only by choosing a former circus rider as his mistress but by allowing his mistress to become an intimate friend of their daughter. The memory of her own rejection by her lover, Paul Monceau, may have sharpened her bitterness.

Gautier wanted to remind them that a family quarrel would do nothing to help find Marie-Thérèse. Instead he said: "Although personally I don't believe your daughter intended to run off with Pontana, it would be unwise to ignore the possibility. I will return to the Sûreté and telegraph the police in Milan to watch in case she should arrive there on any train from Paris."

"Is there nothing more that we can do?"

"Certainly. Pontana is being detained. I will question him and find out whether he had arranged to meet your daughter, either here or in Italy. If we are satisfied he had no such plans, I will contact the commissariat of police in every arrondissement in Paris to find out if they have news of her."

"Do you think she may have been attacked or robbed, even killed?" de Saules asked anxiously.

"It's most unlikely," Gautier replied with a confidence which he certainly did not feel. Violent crime was commonplace in many parts of Paris at night and a girl wandering about on her own would be a tempting target for a savage attack by the apaches of Montmartre or the voyous of Belleville. "If we hear nothing before then, I will arrange for a full-scale search in the morning. In the meantime I have one or two ideas of my own to follow."

"You will keep us informed?"

"Of course."

As Gautier turned to leave the room, he saw that there were two portraits in oils of equal size hanging above the fireplace. One was of Renée de Saules and had been painted when she was a young woman, perhaps twenty years ago. The other was of Marie-Thérèse and must have been executed recently. He wondered whether it might not have been commissioned to mark her eighteenth birthday. Both portraits were clearly the work of the same artist and even allowing for the fact that his style had probably matured during the period between the two paintings, the contrast was remarkable. Renée de Saules, even when she was much younger, had the face of an introvert, the distant, melancholy expression of one who dreams without any real expectation that her dreams will ever be translated into reality. By comparison Marie-Thérèse, although her features were more beautiful, appeared arrogant and self-assertive. And yet, it seemed to Gautier, one could see beneath the arrogance a nervous tension that suggested she was a girl capable of extreme emotions, love and loathing, rage and hysteria.

As he was crossing the room, the doors were

opened by a footman, who came to announce a visitor.

"Monsieur le Comte de Menilmont," he intoned.

The comte hurried in. He was wearing evening dress and carrying his top hat and cane. His manner was outwardly that of a man in haste and anxious, but his movements and gestures still gave an impression of languid indifference. He looked like an actor whose mannerisms and style, stereotyped by long practice, were totally unsuited to the role he was now called upon to play.

Taking the hand of Madame de Saules he kissed it and then bowed slightly to her husband. "Madame, Monsieur, I was not at home when your servant called but I came as soon as I received your message."

"You are very kind, Monsieur le Comte."

"I am only desolate that I cannot help. Have you no news of her?"

"Not as yet."

"At least we know that she is not with that scoundrel Pontana," Madame de Saules remarked.

"Pontana!" de Menilmont exclaimed. "Why should she be with him?"

"I can see you're as surprised as I was," Monsieur de Saules said. "My wife has discovered that Marie-Thérèse has been meeting Pontana in secret. She was afraid that they might have intended to elope."

"You astound me! I didn't even know they had met."

"Pontana must be the reason why she would not consent to become betrothed to you," the banker told the comte.

The footman who had shown the comte into the room was still waiting by the open door and de Menilmont handed him his hat and cane. When he arrived he had seemed to be ready for action, expecting to leave at once and start searching for the missing girl. Now he was prepared to stay and wait until she returned of her own accord or until someone else found her. Could this change of attitude, Gautier wondered, be the result of pique, of a vanity wounded by the knowledge that he had been jilted for an Italian of modest birth?

"How do you know she is not with Pontana?" the comte asked.

"Because he has been arrested and is being detained at the Sûreté," Gautier replied.

"On what charge?"

"He was arrested on the suspicion that he was going to abduct a young woman to Italy. But now he is being held because it is believed that he may have killed the Abbé Didier."

"You cannot be serious!"

Monsieur de Saules confirmed what Gautier had said. "It's the truth."

"Then it's preposterous! Sometimes I think that you policemen are not only stupid but deliberately perverse."

"Do you not believe he might have killed the abbé, Monsieur?" Gautier asked.

"Of course not! Signor Pontana is a poet, a man of intellect and sensitivity, not one of the blackguards and cut-throats and pimps with whom you are accustomed to dealing."

"He is however not an aristocrat."

"What of it?"

"It was you, Monsieur le Comte, who told me that only the aristocracy knew how to treat the clergy."

Gautier was driven to the Sûreté in the same landau that had taken Madame de Saules and himself to the cemetery at Passy two days earlier. Monsieur de Saules had insisted on putting the landau at his disposal for the rest of the evening and for the night if he should need it, to help him in his search for Marie-Thérèse.

On leaving Rue du Bac, Gautier had in mind to go first to the home of the Duchesse de Paiva who, he was certain, had known of the secret meetings between Pontana and Marie-Thérèse and might even have been encouraging them. Then he reasoned that if the duchesse knew where Marie-Thérèse had gone, she would certainly have told her parents when they had telephoned her. Whatever part she may have played in the affair, there was no longer any point in deception. So he went instead to Sûreté headquarters and when he arrived gave instructions that Pontana should be brought up to his office from the cell in which he was being detained. While he was waiting for the Italian to appear, he drafted a telegraph message to the police in Milan and gave instructions for it to be despatched.

Presently Pontana was brought in, escorted by two policemen. Although the evening was hot and airless, he was wearing a belted travelling coat with an astrakhan collar, a tweed suit and brown and white shoes. The humiliation of arrest and his own powerlessness had driven him into a rage which bordered on frenzy, but his flamboyant dress and exaggerated Latin gestures turned drama into comic opera.

As soon as he came in the room and saw Gautier he shouted: "So, it's you! I might have known you were responsible!"

"Responsible for what, Monsieur?"

"The Italian ambassador will hear of this! By what authority do you dare drag me in like a common criminal and lock me up?"

"I am sure the Director-General of the Sûreté explained the reasons for your arrest."

"Oh, yes," Pontana replied bitterly. "Because he thought I was going to abduct the daughter of a rich businessman. You policemen are the same all over the world, just puppets of the rich. Is this why the French Revolution was fought?"

"Are you saying you were not planning to leave the country with Mademoiselle de Saules?"

"Certainly not!"

"In that case who was accompanying you to Italy? You had made two reservations in the wagon-lit."

"My secretary, Ponzi, of course."

"How could he travel with you when he was dead?"

"Dead?"

Gautier had deliberately made the phrasing and timing of his question as brutal as possible to test Pontana, but the Italian's surprise appeared genuine enough. He stared at Gautier disbelievingly.

"Signor Ponzi was found dead in your apartment soon after you had left it. He had been stabbed in much the same way and probably with the same dagger as Abbé Didier."

Slowly Pontana's mind absorbed the implications of what he had heard. The expression on his face was one which Gautier had seen on other faces before; the look of a man suddenly confronted with a situation which is totally unexpected but which he begins to realize could destroy him.

"My God! And you think I killed him?"

"Did you?"

"What possible reason could I have for killing Ponzi? A man who has served me faithfully and well? An old friend?" Impelled by fear, Pontana's words came faster, more urgently. "What could I possibly gain by killing him?"

"Abbé Didier was killed early in the morning," Gautier replied. "It might be that your secretary knew that you left your apartment early on that particular day. When I came and talked to him about the abbé's death, he seemed to become very agitated. Perhaps he realized then that you were implicated in the crime. He may have been prepared to tell the police what he knew."

"I didn't kill the priest, I tell you! Nor did I kill my secretary."

"Can you suggest anyone who might have?"

"No. The man knew scarcely anyone in this country."

"You are acquainted with a Madame Brifout, I believe."

"I know no one of that name."

Gautier took from his pocket the letter which had been found outside Pontana's apartment and showed it to the Italian, explaining where and when it had been discovered. Pontana read the letter, frowning, and it seemed only to increase his bewilderment.

"I have never met this woman and I am not looking for a Scandinavian translator."

"But you are planning to write a drama based on the legends of the Nibelungs?"

"Yes, I am."

"Who knew of your intentions?"

"A few friends."

"The Duchesse de Paiva? Mademoiselle de Saules?"

"Yes and one or two other people."

Gautier took the letter back and returned it to his pocket. He had other questions to ask Pontana about the death of his secretary but they would wait until the morning. His first priority must be to find Marie-Thérèse de Saules. He told Pontana: "I am inclined to believe you when you say you did not kill Signor Ponzi."

"Thank you." The sarcasm in Pontana's remark would have been more effective if it had not been for his obvious relief.

"But I do know for a fact that you have been meeting Mademoiselle de Saules in secret."

"There is no crime in that."

"When did you last see her?"

"Two days ago. On Wednesday in the afternoon." Pontana looked at Gautier, sensing perhaps that he might not have been disposed to believe him and wondering how he could best convince him. He said confidingly: "I may as well admit, Inspector, that the girl and I have been having a mild affair over the past few weeks, but it's all over now. I wrote to her only yesterday morning, saying it would be better if we did not meet again."

"Did she reply to your letter?"

"Yes. I have her note here."

Pontana took a folded piece of notepaper from the breast pocket of his jacket and held it out. As far as one could tell the paper was the same as that on which Madame de Saules had written her note to Abbé Didier. As Gautier unfolded it, he detected the faint smell of an expensive perfume. He felt a sudden revulsion. He did not wish to read a young girl's love letter and had to fight down a mounting contempt for the shabby little adventurer who had handed it to him so readily. Putting his distaste behind him he read what Marie-Thérèse had written.

Monsieur,

I write to say how confused and wounded I feel, both by the message in your letter and by the brutal manner in which it was expressed. After so many declarations on your part and so many promises, I believe that at least I deserve an explanation of your decision that our friendship must come to an end. I hope you will be man enough to give me such an explanation in person and not shelter like a coward behind the written word.

I shall be at our usual rendezvous in the Bois tomorrow morning at seven-thirty. I implore you to be there.

Assuring you that you still have all my devotion,

Marie-Thérèse.

Handing the note back to Pontana, Gautier asked him: "And did you go to this rendezvous yesterday?"

"No. There was nothing to be gained by dragging the affair out." Pontana made it clear that he had no interest in nor concern for the feelings of the girl he had jilted. "You realize, of course, that I could have married her and eventually inherited all the family's wealth."

"Why didn't you?"

"My wife's parents were wealthy aristocrats," Pontana said with the bitterness of one still irritated by unpleasant memories, "and I had to endure their condescension and their slights. I could not face that a second time."

"You prefer to go home and face your creditors?"

"One cannot run away all one's life," Pontana

replied and then added, almost as an after-thought: "Besides, a publisher has made me an excellent offer which will allow me to settle all my debts and live at least in modest comfort."

"And what about Marie-Thérèse? What about her feelings?"

"Only her vanity is hurt. She will recover."

"That note of hers suggests to me that she might be emotionally overwrought."

The Italian poet shrugged his shoulders. "Women love to make these things into a drama. Do you know she once even told me that if she could not spend the rest of her life with me, she would kill herself? What an idea!"

16

AS the Landau moved at a leisurely pace along Quai Voltaire, Gautier looked at the Seine. He often stopped on his way home from the Sûreté at night and leant over the parapet to gaze into the river and to listen to the water lapping against its banks. In the darkness it was no longer a busy thoroughfare, an artery of the city, but a soothing stream, gently washing away the noise and clamour of the day. Tonight the mood of the river was heavy and listless as though it were exhausted after the heat of a long day, and the water seemed scarcely to be moving.

Gautier had sat himself next to the coachman on his box, partly because of the evening's heat and partly because he wished to speak to the man. Jacques was an old family servant, coachman to Monsieur de Saules for twenty-two years and before that first groom and then coachman to the banker's father. His devotion to his master, like that of many loyal servants, had become its own reward.

They spoke of Marie-Thérèse. Even as a little girl, Jacques told Gautier, she had been wilful and imperious, but prone to moods of depression and self-pity whenever she felt she was being harshly or unfairly treated. The coachman recalled an incident that had taken place when she was only five or six years old in her parents' country house. One of the horses in the stables was an ill-tempered beast which even skilled and experienced horsemen did not care to ride. One day when Marie-Thérèse, as a punishment for some naughtiness, had been stopped from going to play with a friend, she had gone to the stables alone, led the horse out and mounted it. The creature had bolted, jumped a wall and thrown her. For several minutes she had lain unconscious, the effects of concussion, but when she eventually recovered from the fall, she had shown no regret.

"You might have been killed," her father had reproached her gently.

"It would have served you right if I had," his daughter had replied, "for being so beastly."

Hearing the story only strengthened the uneasiness which Gautier had felt ever since he had studied the portrait of Marie-Thérèse in her parents' home. Before leaving the Sûreté, he had contacted the police commissariat of every arrondissement in Paris, a task made easier now that they were all connected by telephone. Between them they had no shortage of dead bodies to report; old women found dead in the streets, destroyed by absinthe, young women who had been raped and then strangled, unmarried girls who had poisoned themselves rather than face the shame of pregnancy, married women who had slit their wrists after being abandoned by their husbands, servants and shop-girls and even nuns. But none of their descriptions matched that of Marie-Thérèse de Saules.

In front of him, silhouetted against the night sky, stood the Eiffel Tower. When the tower had been constructed for the Exposition of 1889, it had aroused a raging controversy. An iron tower, 300 metres tall and more than twice as high as any other edifice yet made by man, was a concept that outraged the aesthetes and frightened the timid. It would be a monstrosity, some said, destroying the beauty of Paris. Others, who were supported by mathematicians and engineers, said it could not remain erect and would inevitably collapse. A petition against it being built, signed by many famous people, was sent to the government. Now, not many years later, it was accepted with affection by Parisians as a landmark and by people all over the world as a symbol of the new France which had arisen on the ruins of the war with Germany, a France that led the world in culture and civilization and gaiety.

Seen from below and at night, the tower looked different, a massive, empty structure, silent and inhuman, gaunt and somehow menacing. When the landau pulled up beneath it, they found a policeman from the commissariat of the seventh arrondissement, a young man named Driand, waiting for them. As Gautier had requested over the telephone, he had been to the home of the custodian of the tower who lived nearby and collected the keys to the doors in the four pedestals on which the structure was based.

"Do you think someone is up there?" Driand asked Gautier, nodding towards the summit of the tower.

"There may be."

"The custodian and his men say there was nobody on the tower when they locked up."

"It wouldn't be too difficult to find a hiding-place on either of the first two platforms."

"You should have let me bring one of the mechanics with me to operate the lift."

"If we started one of the lifts, the noise would bring a crowd of people here in no time."

Gautier did not give his real reason for not wanting one of the lifts to be put into operation. If Marie-Thérèse had been on the tower since it had been closed, then it meant she was still not certain whether or not to leap to a spectacular suicide as many Frenchmen had done. The noise of one of the lifts, warning her that people were coming to take her down, might just be enough to push her into a decision.

"I'll come with you, Inspector," Driand offered.

"Thanks. You can help me search the first two platforms. If we find nobody there, I'll climb to the top alone. There's no point in our both going."

They opened the doors in the west pedestal and mounted the stairs which wound their way up through the iron network to the first platform. It was more than sixty metres above the ground, quite high enough to ensure that anyone falling from it would be killed. They could find no one there, nor on the second platform. Leaving

Driand there, Gautier began the slow climb to the third platform at the summit.

He consoled himself with the thought that when the tower was inaugurated on 31st March 1889, Gustave Eiffel had invited the municipal councillors of Paris and a number of other leading notables to ascend the tower and since the lifts were not yet in operation the party had to climb by the stairs. Although most of them ascended only as far as the first platform, more than twenty had managed to reach the top of the tower to hoist the tricolore and drink champagne. What twenty dignitaries, overfed no doubt and out of condition, had managed he should be able to accomplish without too much strain.

As he climbed, the metallic noise of his footsteps seemed to pick up a rhythm of its own like the sound of a hammer being swung in a shipyard. Although at ground level the night had seemed almost suffocatingly still and airless, near the top of the tower he could feel a steady breeze and hear it too, as it made an eerie, whistling sound passing through the network of iron struts. He had an uncomfortable premonition that at any moment a body would fall past him, plummeting to the ground below.

The premonition was false and he found the small platform at the top of the tower was also deserted. He stayed there for a time, regaining his breath and looking down on Paris. Below him was the dark stretch of the Champs de Mars and to the north the dull gleam of the river winding its way through its many bridges. The flickering lights of the city were so faint that he could scarcely make them out. The sensation he felt was not a fear of the height but an intense loneliness, a feeling that he stood there alone, exposed and vulnerable to whatever forces the darkness might conceal.

Repressing a shudder, he began the long climb down to the ground. To occupy his mind as he went, he started wondering what flaw in reasoning had led him to guess, almost to be certain, that he would find Marie-Thérèse de Saules on the Eiffel Tower. If, as he had assumed, she was contemplating killing herself, there were a number of options open to her; poison, opening an artery, a jump into the Seine or from a railway bridge under the wheels of a train. He had discounted them all. If, distraught with grief, she had surrendered to a sudden impulse to end her life, she would have done it by now, in the simplest way and probably in her home. If, on the other hand, suicide was to be a gesture, a protest against life, she would almost certainly have chosen something more spectacular than being dragged out of a river and something less anonymous than finishing as a mutilated body on a railway line. That was the reasoning which had led him to think of the Eiffel Tower.

His deduction had been wrong so he should think again. MarieThérèse had struck him as a girl who could be provoked only too easily into anger. He recalled what Jacques, the coachman, had told him as they had been driving along from the Sûreté. If she were to kill herself it would be a hysterical act of revenge, intended to hurt those who had frustrated her will. If this were the case, one had to wonder whom she was trying to punish. The obvious target was Daniele Pontana who she might think had wronged her. On the other hand she might well imagine that Pontana had abandoned her not of his own will, but because he had been forced to do so by a conspiracy of other people who were determined to wreck their love affair.

By the time he had reached the ground after

his long climb down the tower, he had reached a decision. He told the coachman: "Take me to Notre Dame."

They drove back along the Seine and soon the twin towers of the cathedral came into view. The clouds which had covered the sky earlier in the evening had broken and were dispersing, revealing an almost full moon. In its soft, grey light Notre Dame stood erect and watchful, as though guarding the sleeping city through a tranquil night. They crossed the Ile de la Cité by the Petit Pont and the landau drew to a halt in front of the cathedral.

Gautier went round to the house beside the cathedral where the head verger lived. He knew the man for they had first met two years previously when Gautier was investigating a brutal assault on a woman who worked for one of the canons of the cathedral, and they had met for a glass of wine and a talk two or three times since then. As they worked not far from each other it had been easy to keep up the acquaintanceship.

When Gautier asked him for the keys to the doors to the steps which led up to the cathedral towers, the verger told him: "Both doors have been locked since early evening, Inspector. I do not think you will find anyone up in the towers."

"Even so I would like to go up and look."

"In that case let me come with you."

"No, it will be better if I go alone."

"Whatever you wish, Inspector."

Two flights of stone steps led up to the towers of the cathedral, one on each side just around the corner of the building from the main façade. For no very good reason, Gautier chose the steps on the south side and unlocked the door which opened on to them. The muscles of his calves and thighs were stiff and heavy from the exertion of ascending and descending the Eiffel Tower and as he started to climb the spiral stairs he wondered whether this too would be wasted physical effort. When he reached the top he stepped through the small, pointed watch-tower surmounting the stairs which led on to the roof of the tower. Looking down he could see the landau of Monsieur de Saules with Jacques the coachman standing beside the horses. He imagined he could see the coach-man's face, pale and anxious, looking up towards him.

Moving as quietly as he could, he walked out on to the roof and then stopped abruptly when he saw the figure of a woman sitting on the balustrade with her legs dangling in space. She was sitting near the corner of the balustrade furthest from Gautier so he could not be absolutely certain, but he had the impression that she had only just taken up that position, perhaps because she had heard him climbing the stairs. He took one step towards her.

"Stay where you are or I'll jump!" she called out and he recognized the voice of Marie-Thérèse.

Gautier stopped moving. His first impulse had been to rush across the roof and grab the girl, but he reasoned that if she had been on the tower for several hours without making up her mind to kill herself, then it was unlikely that she would choose that precise moment to do so. She would talk first, he felt certain.

Slowly and as casually as he could, he took a cigar from his breast pocket and lit it. He was not a regular smoker but liked an occasional cigar after a meal, and earlier that evening in the café in Place Dauphine the daughter Janine had given him one with the compliments of the establishment. Before he had time to smoke it, Surat had come into the café to tell him of Ponzi's death.

"Who are you?" Marie-Thérèse called out.

"Inspector Gautier."

"So you're another one," she said bitterly.

"Another one?"

"In the pay of my mother."

"What makes you think that?"

"You have come on her behalf, haven't you? To find me and persuade me to return home."

"I don't see why you should assume that."

"Merde to you!" she shouted suddenly. "And merde too to all her other lackeys, the clergy, the police!"

Her voice which had seemed calm and controlled at first, rose shrilly to a pitch that suggested hysteria. She began to swear, using a string of oaths which one might have thought would be unknown to young ladies of Paris society. Gautier sensed that she had been saving up her anger and was venting it on him simply because he was the first person to confront her. He wondered what he should do or say. His police training had included no instruction on how to deal with potential suicides.

"Foutez-vous!" she screamed. "Nothing you can say is going to stop me jumping."

"You must do as you please, Mademoiselle," Gautier said, impulsively deciding on his

264

strategy. "If you do kill yourself it may even save me a great deal of work."

"What do you mean?"

"Suicide could only be an admission of guilt and then perhaps your accomplice would confess."

"Accomplice? What are you talking about?"

"Pontana is being held by us on suspicion of unlawful killing. His secretary, Signor Ponzi, was found stabbed to death earlier this evening. But then you must be aware of all this, Mademoiselle."

Marie-Thérèse stared at him. He was not close enough to her to see the expression on her face and thus to decide whether she was astonished or puzzled or suspicious. She said nothing, so Gautier continued: "We arrested Pontana at the Gare de Lyon. He had reservations on the night train to Milan and was waiting for his travelling companion."

"That can only have been his secretary," she said slowly.

"Dead men don't need a berth in the wagon-lit. No, Mademoiselle, we believe it was you for whom he was waiting."

"Well it was not, I can tell you that." Her denial was bitter.

"It might possibly have been another woman, I suppose."

"Why should you have thought it was me?" Marie-Thérèse asked. Her hysteria had subsided and one could see that she was starting to think about the implications of what Gautier had told her.

"Because we knew you and Pontana had formed, shall we call it a liaison, that you were meeting him alone in the Bois de Boulogne and in the house of the Duchesse de Paiva."

"That means you were having him followed," she remarked quickly. "Why should you have been doing that even before his secretary was murdered? Because my mother paid you to, of course."

"Your mother has nothing to do with it," Gautier replied patiently. "As you know, I have been investigating the killing of Abbé Didier."

"What possible connection could there be between the abbé and Daniele?"

"We know that he went to see the abbé not long before his death and quarrelled with him violently."

"So you suspect him of two murders?"

"They could be related."

"That's crazy!"

"Abbé Didier was killed early in the morning. Ponzi was living in the same apartment as Pontana and he might have been able to testify that he left the place at an unusual hour on the day."

Gautier sensed that although Marie-Thérèse did not believe that Pontana had killed two men, she was beginning to think of him and of their affair in a different light. Finally she said: "Whatever Daniele may have done, you can be assured that I was not his accomplice."

"Then why did you come up here?"

He half expected that she would tell him that her behaviour was no concern of his. Instead she gave a short, bitter laugh. "Because our liaison, as you term it, is at an end. Daniele is abandoning me." Gautier made no comment so she added: "Do you find that hard to believe?"

"Not necessarily. It confirms his story."

"What story?"

"When I questioned him this evening at the Sûreté, he told me the affair was over. He also showed me a letter which he says you wrote to him."

"He showed you the letter?"

"Yes. The one in which you asked him to meet you once more in the Bois." Gautier had not intended to mention the letter. He used it now as a piece of calculated shock treatment, hoping it would discredit the Italian more than anything he could say to denigrate him. "The fellow was desperate, I suppose, to prove it was not you but his secretary he was waiting for at the railway station."

"Yes, that would be in character."

"So you see, killing yourself will solve nothing. Pontana needs your help."

"And if I give it to him he may not return to Italy. Is that what you are suggesting?"

"I cannot say what he is likely to do."

"I think I might reconcile myself to life without him," she replied with sarcasm.

"In that case why are you contemplating suicide?" Gautier was sure now that her mood had changed. Hysterical rage had been replaced by a cold but lucid anger. He asked: "Who are you trying to punish? The people who interfered in your life? Your mother? The Church?"

"They deserve to suffer," Marie-Thérèse said angrily.

"Possibly, but would they? From what you say you and your mother are not on the closest of terms. As for the Church, the abbé is dead. You cannot reach him." He paused, giving her

268

time to consider his arguments and then added: "As I see it, the only person you would be hurting would be your father."

Marie-Thérèse did not reply, but sat motionless on the parapet of the tower, staring out over the city. A breeze had sprung up and was driving scattered clouds across the sky which, as they passed over the moon, threw shadows across the roof-tops. Gautier began to fear that a sudden gust might unbalance the girl from her precarious seat on the balustrade and send her hurtling to the cobblestones almost seventy metres below. Resisting once again an impulse to go and pull her to safety, he waited. There was nothing more that he could usefully say or do. After what seemed like an age, she turned towards him.

"You are right," she said slowly and calmly, and then added with the assurance of one accustomed to giving orders: "Will you help me to get down?"

As they felt their way haltingly down the dark stairs, Gautier felt himself shiver. He wondered why. The girl meant nothing to him. She was spoilt and self-willed and proud. At that very moment no doubt there were a score of people facing death in Paris, from a drunken husband's

269

hands, an apache's knife or a bottle of poison, whose lives his time would be better spent in saving. Quite possibly Marie-Thérèse had never really intended suicide and would have come down from the tower of the cathedral of her own accord. Even so, knowing all this, now that the tension was over leaving him drained and weak, he felt an enormous relief.

"Are you going to take me to the Sûreté?" Marie-Thérèse asked.

"No. I believe what you have told me. I'll take you home. Tomorrow no doubt we'll find out who killed Signor Ponzi."

Together they crossed the square in front of Notre Dame towards the waiting carriage. As they drew near the coachman, he stepped forward, grabbed Marie-Thérèse's hands and tried to kiss them. His eyes were full of tears. Marie-Thérèse looked at him, seemingly astonished, for a moment and Gautier thought she was going to rebuke him. Then she pulled her hands away and embraced the old man affectionately.

They drove towards Rue du Bac and for several minutes neither Marie-Thérèse nor Gautier spoke. Then she said wonderingly, as though she were speaking aloud to herself:

"Ever since I was a child I've ordered Jacques about, bullied him, showed him no consideration. And yet he really cares what happens to me!"

As Gautier climbed the three flights of stairs to his apartment, a clock chimed half-past twelve. Now that the day was over, he felt a great weariness. He could not even begin to calculate how many steps he had climbed and descended since morning.

The awareness of his fatigue brought, as it often did for him, thoughts of sex; not erotic fantasies nor even a clear and precise desire for a woman, but a chain of images all associated with or linked to sex. He had noticed more than once the deeper satisfaction he found in making love when he was physically exhausted after a long and tiring day. Remembering this he also recalled how he had looked at the voluptuous body of Janine in her café in Place Dauphine and wondered whether she was now in bed and alone. He remembered too the suggestive invitation of the Duchesse de Paiva and wondered whether or not he regretted having declined it. And even while he was thinking, he realized that his thoughts were no more than an evasion, an escape from the knowledge that upstairs nothing waited for him except an empty apartment and an empty bed.

For once life proved him wrong. When he opened the door to the apartment, he saw that the gas light in the hallway was burning. One evening not many months ago, he had arrived home to find that light burning and had divined correctly that Suzanne was there. He had also assumed with mixed feelings that she had returned to live with him and then learned that she had only come to tell him she was setting up a ménage with another man. If she was here now, he reasoned gloomily, it could only mean trouble; not trouble with money because her father had plenty, but trouble in the café which she ran with her lover, the kind of trouble that needed a policeman's help to solve.

He went into the living-room and found not Suzanne but Juliette, stretched out in an armchair. In his surprise all he could think of saying was: "How did you get in?"

"I told your concierge I was your younger sister, that I had come to visit you but that we had missed each other at the railway station."

"And she believed you?"

"If she didn't believe my story then she must have believed the five francs I offered her."

He thought he could detect a subtle change in her appearance and manner since their last meeting. In an indefinable way she seemed more feminine and more appealing and yet he could see nothing in her dress or hair-style to explain the change.

He did not ask her why she had come, thinking it would be gauche to do so, but she answered his unspoken question: "I'm here to finish what I didn't even start last night. Are you going to turn me away?"

She stood up and faced him and Gautier felt the slow, familiar surge of desire. Reaching out he placed his hands gently on her shoulders. She flinched perceptibly and he thought she was going to back away, but she smiled nervously, a banal smile.

The only remark she could find to make was banal too.

"I don't know how to begin."

17

GAUTIER had often noticed that certain sensations, once familiar but buried deep in his memory—the taste of a particular dish he had eaten as a child, a phrase of music, an unusual pattern of contrasting colours—aroused in him not a recollection of past events but emotions with which those sensations had been unconsciously but strongly associated, wonderment or delight or even a totally irrational fear.

And so it was that as he was awakening next morning, the smell of coffee drifting into the bedroom brought with it a sense of contentment and well-being, the knowledge that he could continue to lie in bed with his eyes closed for a few more precious minutes, listening to Suzanne as she moved around the kitchen, thinking of the day ahead and savouring the satisfactions and the challenges it would bring. Then he remembered that it was not Suzanne in the kitchen and that it could only be Juliette.

Presently she came into the bedroom carrying

two cups of coffee, fresh croissants and butter on a tray. She was wearing one of his cotton nightshirts, which she had to hold hitched up to prevent it trailing on the ground and in which, for some inexplicable reason, she reminded him of an orphan.

"Do you really wear garments like this one?" she asked.

"Never. They are only a fire precaution."

"A fire precaution?"

"I sleep naked but one must have something to put on if the building were to catch fire."

"Have you ever thought of pyjamas?"

"Certainly not! Do you take me for a radical?"

They both laughed. Pyjamas had only recently been introduced to France, having been invented, some said, by the British in India and they were mistrusted by the conservative bourgeoisie. People hinted that they were unhygienic and could even be dangerous.

"You didn't go downstairs dressed like that to fetch the bread, did you?" Gautier asked her.

"No, the concierge brought it up."

"How much did you say you gave her as a pourboire?"

"I suspect she only came up to see if you

were having an incestuous affair with your sister!"

Juliette sat cross-legged on the bed and set the breakfast tray down between them. Gautier looked at her as she poured the coffee. Now that most of the barriers that had existed between them had crumbled, he was enjoying her candour, her habit of tossing off unconventional remarks and even her probing, personal questions. No one had ever treated him in quite the same way before.

As though to confirm this assessment of her, Juliette suddenly asked him: "How did I make love last night?"

"Like a virgin." Gautier smiled to show there was no malice in his answer.

What he said was true. She had at first been unresponsive to his love-making, accepting it not frigidly but nervously, as though each caress were a new experience to be received with caution. And even as the gradual discovery of pleasure melted her reserve, she had returned the caresses inexpertly and with diffidence.

"Until last night," she replied, "I was a virgin in everything but name."

"What about your marriage?"

"That was a fiasco. Would you like me to tell you about it?"

"Only if you want to," he replied, sensing that she did.

She told him the story of her marriage, simply and without embellishment as a good writer should and without embarrassment. As a young girl, she explained, she had been slow to mature. Her leisure had been divided between riding and athletic pursuits in which she had been encouraged by her father and books for which she had found she had an insatiable appetite. She had taken little interest in men and none in marriage. When she was twenty and still single, her father had begun to grow concerned. As her mother was by this time dead and his own health was deteriorating, he feared that she might be left alone and unprotected.

Eventually to please him she had agreed to marry a Spanish gentleman of good birth, but she had stipulated and her bridegroom had agreed that it would be a marriage of convenience and nothing more. Don Nicolas Gonzales y Ribeiro was in financial difficulties and in return for a handsome dowry was ready to promise that their relationship should remain platonic. On the night of their wedding, however, forgetting his promises, he had decided to take what every Spaniard would regard as his rights and when Juliette had refused him, he had broken down the bedroom door and tried to take them by force. Next morning she had sent for her father. The General had arrived, horsewhipped the cowardly Spaniard and taken his daughter away.

"It was my fault really," Juliette concluded, "a piece of conceit. With the arrogance of youth I thought I could impose my own terms on life."

"And you have kept away from men ever since?"

"It was an experience I did not want to repeat."

"Not even with Daniele Pontana?"

She frowned. "Pontana?"

"You once told me that he had made you a proposition."

"Don't remind me of it!" Juliette said and laughed. "That was the most outrageous example of masculine vanity I have ever known!"

"What did he propose?"

"He told me very seriously that I could never

be a truly great writer until I had experienced the emotions of a great love affair and that there was no one better qualified than he to teach me about love."

"I don't believe it!"

"That was not all. He said that if I let him move in with me in my house, we could have the love affair of the century and I would be the envy of every woman in Paris."

"The fellow is a caricature," Gautier exclaimed. "A caricature Casanova."

"Of course there was a price to pay," Juliette went on. "Poets, he pointed out, were not as ordinary people or even ordinary writers. They must live in an environment that would inspire their muse, surrounded by beauty and not bothered with the sordid necessities of life, especially not with money. A rich Russian lady, he claimed, had offered him an allowance of sixty thousand francs a year if he would live with her. But she was middle-aged and ugly, while I am young and desirable. So he would be my lover for only a mere fifty thousand francs a year."

"You cannot be serious!"

"It's true! Every word!"

When they had stopped laughing, Gautier

said: "Perhaps you should have asked him for a sample of what he had to offer; on approval as it were."

Reaching out she touched his cheek lightly. "Nothing could have been better than last night." Her eyes appeared to cloud over but not with sadness. "Will we make love again?"

"I hope so."

"When?"

He looked at her, imagining the contours of her body beneath the nightshirt, remembering the firmness of her breasts, the smoothness of her stomach and the movements of her hips as she had lain in bed with him only a few hours before. His reluctance to become involved with Juliette had vanished now that he was beginning to understand her.

"Why not now?" he asked her gently. "We have time."

Later that morning they stood outside her house in Rue Jacob. They had walked there from his apartment because Juliette had wished to, strolling in the morning sunshine, passing from the fifteenth arrondissement where he lived to the seventh, crossing first Boulevard du Montparnasse and then Rue Babylone into the Faubourg

St. Germain. The streets of the Faubourg were quieter than usual, for many of the families who lived there had left Paris for the country during the past week. Almost the only people to be seen in the streets were priests, which might have given the impression one was in Rome.

For Gautier the main pleasure of the morning was that he had completely forgotten his work and the Sûreté. Juliette and he had talked of other things; books, the theatre, the rights of women, the perfidious British, a possible alliance with Russia. The sight of the priests hurrying through the streets reminded him, however, that the death of Abbé Didier remained unsolved.

"Do you by any chance know a Madame Brifout?" he asked Juliette suddenly.

"That's an odd question!"

"Why odd?"

"Madame Brifout was a character I created in my last novel but one. So far as I know there is no woman of the same name in real life."

"It is an unusual name."

"Yes it is, deliberately so. Ever since an unfortunate experience which I had when I was just beginning to write, I have always chosen unusual names for my characters. That lessens the chances of people taking offence because they believe you are writing about them."

She told Gautier how in her first novel she had named one of the characters as the Comte d'Albi. The character was supposed to be the leader of a group of people committed to defying and ultimately destroying current social convention and Juliette had chosen the title Albi because of its association with the Albigensians and therefore its connotations of heresy.

"So I was astounded," she told Gautier, "when I received a violent and abusive letter from the Comte de Menilmont. What I did not know is that his full name is Comte Raymond d'Albi de Menilmont. He accused me of trying to mock his ancestors."

"What did you do? Apologize?"

"Certainly not! Why should I have? No, I brought the affair to a speedy conclusion by challenging the comte to a duel."

"That was courageous! He has the reputation of being a fine swordsman."

"So am I. But anyway I knew he would never agree to fight a woman."

"What happened?"

"He was terrified that if the news of my challenge spread he would be made to look ridiculous. So it was he who apologized for his letter, and we agreed to forget the whole affair."

They were standing outside Juliette's house, neither of them it seemed wishing to end the conversation. Gautier realized however that on a normal day he would by that time have been at work for at least two hours. He knew also that Courtrand would be expecting two reports from him that morning, one on the killing of Ponzi and the other describing how Marie-Thérèse de Saules had been found and taken safely home, and there was a call he wished to make before he wrote the reports.

When she realized he was about to leave, Juliette said: "Will I see you again today?"

"I would like that. When?"

"We could have an aperitif together before lunch. I have an article to write but that must be finished and sent round to the newspaper before mid-day."

"Then let's say we will meet at twelve fifteen."

"Agreed. We'll go to a café. You won't mind that, will you?"

"Of course not. Which café?"

"You may choose. Take me to the café where

you usually go. I'll be waiting for you here at twelve fifteen."

Gautier walked up to the Seine and boarded an omnibus which took him along the river before crossing into Place de la Concorde and from there turning into Avenue des Champs Elysées. A fiacre would have accomplished the journey more quickly but he needed a little time to plan what he was going to say to the Duchesse de Paiva. So he sat on the upper deck in the sunshine as the horses drew the vehicle along at their leisurely pace.

When he reached the duchesse's house, the footman who opened the door was unwilling to admit him, saying that his mistress never received visitors before mid-day. Gautier told the man who he was and that he should inform his mistress that the Inspector had important news for her. The footman went away and returned soon afterwards to show him to the same room in which Gautier and the duchesse had talked the previous evening. She was waiting for him, dressed today in a gown of pale green silk. Her dark hair was taken up and pinned in tight curls to her head, showing that the lines of her throat and chin were still firm and youthful. When Gautier had last seen her she had seemed voluptuous and seductive. Now her looks and her manner were those of a proud eighteenth-century beauty.

"What is this news you have for me, Inspector, that cannot wait until a civilized hour?" Her tone was mocking but there was anxiety in her eyes.

"I thought you should know that Signor Pontana was arrested last night."

"Arrested? How could he be arrested? He has committed no crime."

"That remains to be seen. His secretary, Signor Ponzi, was found stabbed to death in their apartment last night and Pontana was arrested before he could board a train for Italy."

"He was planning to go home last night in any case," the duchesse protested.

"How do you know that?" Gautier asked. She turned away, saying nothing and he noticed her hands tighten their grip on the arms of her chair. He continued: "That was the reason you tried to keep me here last night, was it not? You knew Pontana was leaving and you wanted to make sure that I would not stop him?" Still she did not speak and mildly irritated by her silence he said: "If it transpires that he did kill

Ponzi, the consequences could be serious for you, Madame."

"I know nothing of Ponzi," she replied brusquely. "I thought you might try to stop Daniele leaving because you suspected him of killing the abbé."

"As it happens I believe you," Gautier replied. "I believe you paid Pontana half a million francs to go home. That was why you sold your necklace. You gave him the money on condition that he went back to Italy and left Marie-Thérèse de Saules alone. The story you told me about having an illegitimate daughter was a pure fabrication."

Gautier did not tell her that he had never believed what she had told him about a daughter mainly because she had borrowed too freely from another story which many people in Paris still remembered. When the actress Sarah Bernhardt had given birth, while unmarried, to a son, she had told the world that the father was a Belgian of royal blood, the Prince de Ligne. In Sarah's story her prince too had wished to marry but, realizing that his family would disown him, she had made a sacrifice of her love and refused.

"And I suppose your real reason for going to

286

see Abbé Didier was that you had heard or guessed he was making enquiries about Pontana through the Church in Italy. You asked him to stop because you had a better way to get rid of the Italian." The duchesse turned away once more and said nothing, so Gautier continued: "It would be better if you were frank with me."

"All right," she said at last. "All of what you have said is true. I did give Daniele money to go away. Was I wrong in trying to save a girl from an unscrupulous and cynical adventurer, a man twenty years older than her who is losing his hair and losing his teeth and is only interested in her money?"

"I am sure you acted from the best of motives, but in my experience women prefer to find out these things for themselves. As it happens your attempt to save Marie-Thérèse almost had the opposite effect."

"What do you mean?"

"She was found late last night up on one of the towers of Notre Dame where she had gone to kill herself."

The duchesse stared at Gautier in disbelief. Then she turned white and moaned and seemed about to faint. He stepped forward, meaning to assist her, but after shutting her eyes tightly as though to concentrate her physical resources, she recovered and sat erect in her chair.

"Marie-Thérèse is safe," Gautier told her. "She was persuaded to come down from the tower."

"I had to act." The duchesse appeared not to have heard what he had said. "The man is a scoundrel. He even offered to be my lover if I consented to make him a generous allowance."

"Perhaps you should have told Marie-Thérèse that."

"Such is her infatuation that she would not have believed me. But what Pontana really wants is to go home, to pay off his debts, to live in style and cock a snook at his dead wife's relatives."

"So you know his wife is dead?"

"Yes. He told Marie-Thérèse and me in the strictest confidence. He did not want people in France to know he was unattached."

"So I believe. In case too many women set their caps at him."

"You may be sarcastic if you wish, but he is very attractive to women."

"Anyway I do not believe he killed the abbé. Soon he will be released and will be able to make his triumphant return to Venice."

Gautier's words did nothing to reassure the duchesse. Rising from her chair, she crossed to the window of the room and looked out over the Avenue des Champs Elysées. Gautier was astonished to notice how her appearance had changed during the last few minutes. Now she was no longer the handsome eighteenth-century beauty but a miserable, frightened woman approaching middle age.

"You were right," she said gloomily. "I should never have interfered."

"No real harm has been done, except possibly to a girl's vanity."

"But what if she finds out that I gave Daniele the money? She would blame me for ruining her romance. She would never speak to me again."

"I doubt that."

"Yes. I know Marie-Thérèse. It would be the end of my friendship and you can have no idea how much that means to me."

Gautier realized that she was looking for another kind of assurance. He said: "You can be assured that I will not tell her what I know and of the sacrifice which you made for her."

"Do I have your promise, Jean-Paul?"

"Yes. Neither will I tell her father."

Anger flared in her eyes at his calculated

piece of impertinence, but only for a moment. Then she looked at him appreciatively and laughed. "You and I understand each other, I can see that."

Unlocking the drawer of the table in his office, Gautier took out the copy of *Mytilène* which had been found in Abbé Didier's room. The note which Madame de Saules had written to the abbé was still between the pages where he had first found it. Unfolding it, he read what Madame de Saules had written once again. There was only one small point which he wished to verify and when he had done that he returned the note to its place in the book and the book to the drawer.

Then he sat down and wrote the two reports which Courtrand would be expecting from him. The first was brief; little more than a statement that Mademoiselle de Saules had been discovered at Notre Dame Cathedral and taken home to her parents. The second was an account of the circumstances in which the body of Ponzi had been found and the enquiries that were being made to trace his assailant. Gautier never gave more detail than he had to in his reports, partly because writing reports made him bored and impatient but also because the less Courtrand knew about an investigation the less he was likely to interfere.

As he was finishing the second report, Surat came into the room. He had the air of a man with news of importance to report. Surat could never conceal his pleasure when any investigation which Gautier initiated produced results.

"We're in luck, Patron," he said. "Bastat has found a fiacre driver who picked up a woman in a veil in Rue du Cherche-Midi just after seven forty last evening. The man is fairly certain that the woman came out of the building where Pontana has his apartment."

"Where did he take her?"

"To the Hotel Cavour in Rue St. Denis."

"Do we know the place?"

"It's one of the many disreputable hotels in that area; a hotel de rendezvous. The management have been in a little trouble with the police from time to time. Apparently it is frequented by homosexuals of both sexes."

"Tell Bastat to get along there and find out as much as he can about this mysterious lady. The owner of the hotel won't want to talk, of course, but tell Bastat to stand no nonsense. If necessary he can bring the man in for questioning."

"I'll see to it immediately. And is there anything you wish me to do?"

"There is as a matter of fact. I want you to send an anonymous message."

18

WHEN Gautier arrived at the home of Monsieur de Saules in Rue du Bac, he saw Courtrand's carriage waiting in the courtyard in front of the house. It did not particularly surprise him that the Director-General should have decided to call on the banker before going to the Sûreté. Courtrand would be anxious to learn whether Marie-Thérèse had been found the previous night or, a less charitable possibility, he might already have found out that Gautier had succeeded in his mission to find the girl and have come to take the credit. Whatever the reason, Gautier was not displeased because it suited his plan to have Courtrand there.

The footman who opened the door led him to a small drawing-room on the first floor at the back of the house which was reserved for use in the mornings. As he passed through other rooms, he noticed that much of the furniture had been covered with dust-sheets and two manservants were taking down the pictures. In the small drawing-room Courtrand was talking to Monsieur and Madame de Saules. His beard was freshly trimmed, his moustaches neatly waxed and Gautier guessed that he had been visited by his barber that morning.

"We were just telling Monsieur Courtrand," the banker said to Gautier after welcoming him, "that my wife and I will always be indebted to you for what you did last night."

"I knew you could rely on Gautier." Courtrand seemed in a generous mood. "That was why I chose him as the man to help you."

"How is the demoiselle this morning?" Gautier asked.

"Asleep and tranquil. The doctor gave her a sleeping draught. We were planning to leave for our house in the country on Monday, but we have brought our departure forward to this afternoon."

"I am sure that's wise," Courtrand said. "A few days in the country, repose, fresh air and new companions and she will soon forget this nightmare."

Monsieur de Saules continued talking animatedly, telling Courtrand and Gautier of his plans for the summer and for their daughter, of their house in the country, of the customs of the region, of processions and fêtes and folklore. His wife said little. Even so, although she did not show the same delight as her husband in knowing that Marie-Thérèse was safe, Gautier could sense behind her natural reserve a satisfaction that critical observers might have read as complacency.

Gautier was content to listen to Monsieur de Saules and even to encourage him with questions and a show of interest. He was like an actor improvising and playing for time because one of the leading characters in the play was late in making his entrance. Courtrand, on the other hand, was beginning to appear politely restless, as though he were conscious that he and Gautier might be outstaying their welcome.

Finally he said: "Madame, Monsieur, I am delighted all is well with your daughter, but we have imposed on you too long. I know you have many preparations to make for your journey to the country."

"For my part I am glad to have been of service last night," Gautier said, deciding that he must buy at least a little more time, "but in truth I came to see you this morning for another reason."

"What was that?"

"As you know I am investigating the death of Abbé Didier. I hoped perhaps that you, Madame, might be able to help me."

Courtrand looked apprehensive, nervous that Gautier was about to do or say something which might offend the banker and his wife and so embarrass himself. He said sharply: "I cannot see how Madame or Monsieur could possibly help you."

"With respect, Monsieur, we know that Madame de Saules was a very close friend of the abbé."

"If I can be of any help," Madame de Saules told Gautier, "you only have to tell me how."

"The secretary of Signor Pontana was killed last night."

"But that is dreadful!"

"We have strong reasons for believing that he was killed by the same person who stabbed the abbé in his church."

"Could that not have been Pontana?" Courtrand asked. "You told me you suspected him of killing the abbé."

"I think not. Pontana left his apartment in a calm and leisurely way, stopped at a tailor's establishment to collect two suits he had ordered and then waited for some time at the

Gare de Lyon. That is scarcely the behaviour of a man who has just stabbed another man to death."

"The Italians are known for their callous, carefully planned murders. Look at the Borgias," Courtrand said and then added: "But I really cannot imagine why you should think Madame can help you in this affair."

For the past few minutes, Gautier had been extemporizing, talking merely to prolong the conversation. When he left the Sûreté, he had not expected to find Courtrand at the home of Monsieur de Saules, but now he wished to keep him there a little longer. Although he felt no real resentment at the occasional undeserved reprimands and petty slights which he had to endure from his chief, it would give him a kind of perverse pleasure if Courtrand were to witness the climax of the scheme he had put into operation that morning. As it happened he was spared the necessity of improvising any further, because at that moment the Comte de Menilmont came into the room.

He arrived as he had done the previous evening announced by a footman, but this time there was a perceptible difference in his manner. Behind the inbred aloofness and studied air of ennui one could plainly detect a genuine anxiety. He could scarcely wait to finish the formality of shaking hands.

Then he blurted out: "Where is she?"

"Marie-Thérèse? She is still in bed," Madame de Saules replied.

"But you have come to arrest her?" The comte looked at Courtrand.

"Arrest Mademoiselle de Saules! Whatever gave you that idea?"

"I received an anonymous message that the police were about to arrest her for complicity in the killing of the Italian Ponzi."

"You have obviously been the victim of a joke," Monsieur de Saules remarked. "And a joke in very poor taste."

"The Inspector believes we may be able to help his enquiries into the death of Abbé Didier," Madame de Saules said quietly; so quietly that Gautier wondered whether the remark might be intended as a message to the comte or a warning.

"I have been thinking about what you told us last night," de Menilmont said to Gautier, "and I have come to the conclusion that you may be right. Perhaps it was Pontana who killed the abbé."

"Gautier thinks the abbé was murdered by the same person who killed Pontana's secretary."

"Pontana could have killed them both."

"That is what Monsieur Courtrand believes."

"What motive could he possibly have for killing his secretary?" Gautier posed the question deliberately, as a chess player makes a seemingly innocuous manoeuvre to start a chain of moves that will develop his chosen line of strategy.

"Is it true that Abbé Didier was killed early one morning?" the comte asked.

"Yes. At a little before seven o'clock, we believe."

"Ponzi was living in the same apartment as his employer. They had no servants. He might well have seen or heard Pontana leave the apartment early on the morning when the abbé was killed."

"A faultless piece of deduction, Monsieur le Comte," Courtrand said. "Ponzi might easily have been the only person who could have given evidence that would have incriminated his master. And did you not report, Gautier, that the abbé had received Pontana's confession in his church on a previous occasion?"

"Apparently so."

"In that case Pontana would have already knelt in the confessional and seen how he would be able to stab the abbé through the lattice of the screen."

"I find it hard to understand nevertheless," Monsieur de Saules observed, "why he should wish to kill the abbé."

"Because he did not trust him," Courtrand replied. "He was afraid the abbé would tell other people what he had learnt about his life in Italy."

"What had he learnt?"

"That Pontana had a thoroughly unsavoury reputation," de Menilmont said.

"And he left Italy mainly because it was rumoured that he had killed his wife," Courtrand added.

"Killed his wife! What sort of monster is he?"

"If that had been generally known, he would never have been admitted to a single drawing-room in Paris," Madame de Saules said indignantly and then, turning towards her husband, she added: "And do you still blame me for trying to prevent our daughter from associating with him?"

They have the wretch half way to the guillotine already, Gautier thought. The eagerness with which Madame de Saules, the comte and Courtrand were seizing on every circumstantial detail, every piece of hearsay or rumour that would incriminate Pontana would have been distasteful if it had not been frightening. One recognized animal instinct, the herd banding together, rejecting the outsider and preparing to slaughter him.

"For my part, I do not believe that Pontana killed his secretary," he said slowly, measuring his words not for effect but to make sure the others would listen to him. "I believe the reason why Ponzi was killed is exactly the opposite to what Monsieur le Comte has suggested."

The four people in the room stared at him. Courtrand said angrily: "What on earth do you mean? You're talking in riddles, man!"

"Ponzi might equally have been killed because he was the only person who could state that Pontana had definitely not killed the abbé, that he was in bed in their apartment that morning when the stabbing took place."

"That doesn't make sense."

"What the Inspector is implying"—Madame

de Saules was the first to understand the suggestions of what Gautier had said—"is that someone wanted Pontana to be accused of the crime, that they wanted to make sure he could not prove his innocence."

"I've been told many times," Gautier continued calmly, "you have all told me that it is impossible to imagine how anyone would wish to kill such a kind, saintly man as Abbé Didier. We know that Mademoiselle de Saules resented what she thought was his interference in her life; we know that Juliette Prévot was angry with him because he condemned her books and probably was instrumental in losing her the Prix Fémina; Madame Trocville sneered at him because she thought he turned people away from her salon during the Dreyfus affair, but all these were petty feelings of resentment and annoyance."

"What about Pontana?" the Comte de Menilmont interrupted.

Gautier ignored him and continued: "One cannot imagine that anyone would kill a priest for such trivial reasons. I believe that whoever killed Abbé Didier had no personal feelings of animosity towards him. I believe the abbé was killed with the sole purpose of implicating

Pontana, so that even if the evidence were not strong enough to get him convicted and guillotined, he would be disgraced."

"What a preposterous idea!" Courtrand exclaimed. "Who would do such a thing?"

"What we have heard from witnesses suggests that both the abbé and Ponzi were killed by a mysterious lady in a veil. I know of only one woman who was doing everything she could to discredit Pontana, who wanted him exposed, who wanted to be rid of him." Gautier stopped speaking and looked directly at Madame de Saules.

"Are you accusing me?" she asked quietly.

"Have you gone mad, Gautier?" Courtrand shouted. Such was his fury that his beard and moustaches seemed to quiver and his face had the deep flush of imminent apoplexy.

"Some mothers would not think it too drastic a remedy to save a daughter," Gautier said evenly, but then he smiled. "No, Madame, I do not believe for one moment that you would ever be capable of two brutal murders."

"Of course she isn't!" Monsieur de Saules said.

"On the other hand, what if the assassin were not a woman, but a man in disguise?" Gautier paused, this time to allow his audience time to realize the significance of what he was about to say. "In that event, Monsieur le Comte, it could only have been you."

No one spoke. Even Courtrand was silent, realizing now that this was the accusation which Gautier had intended all along to make and that he would scarcely make it without being sure of his facts. The Comte de Menilmont's lips twitched in a smile of contempt, but apart from that he betrayed no sign of any emotion, or surprise or anger.

"One has to admire your imagination, Inspector," he said coolly. "You should have been a novelist."

"I do not merit your compliment, Monsieur," Gautier replied. "Nothing I have ever conceived would match the imagination of your plan to destroy Pontana. You knew he had quarrelled with Abbé Didier. In one sense you might even be said to have provoked him into the quarrel by prevailing on Madame de Saules to persuade the abbé to make enquiries about Pontana in Italy. Possibly you may even have let slip to the Duchesse de Paiva that these enquiries were being made, knowing she was likely to tell Pontana. You would know that the

Italian was already hostile to the Church for the way it had treated him. And once Pontana had lost his temper with the abbé, the rest of your plan was really quite simple to execute."

"Perfectly simple!" The comte's sarcasm was intended to shrivel. "I make a habit of killing a few priests from time to time."

"You went to the church one morning and saw that it would be quite easy to kill the abbé in the shelter of the confessional. And a few days later you went there again and killed him."

Gautier was aware that the de Saules and Courtrand were looking only at him and never once glanced at the comte. It was as though they were determined not to turn their heads nor to shift their gaze, afraid that if they did they might be embarrassed by seeing guilt in the comte's face.

"You would not even stop there," Gautier continued. "No doubt you considered that we in the Sûreté would be too obtuse to see what we were supposed to see. So on each occasion when you met me, you first praised Pontana and then dropped a subtle hint that would plant suspicion of him in my mind. At Madame Trocville's you told me of his skill in the classical art of Italian duelling, in which I

305

understand a dagger is used as well as a sword. You even managed to slip in a reference to the fact that a book of his had been banned by the Vatican. Then on the night when we went to the circus, you reminded me of his flair for impersonating women. I suppose it may even have been you who suggested to Pontana that he impersonate Sarah Bernhardt when he read his poem at Madame Trocville's soirée. You also made a remark about his collection of medieval weapons which included of course a set of daggers."

"Apparently you can find a devious meaning in everything I say."

"I believe you are a man who leaves nothing to chance, but like all of us you are fallible. You never checked to make sure that Ponzi was living in a hotel as he pretended. It must have been an unpleasant shock at the duchesse's house that evening when you learnt he was using the maid's room in Pontana's apartment. You realized at once that he might be able to prove Pontana's innocence. So the next evening you went to the apartment, dressed in a woman's clothes and armed with a letter of introduction you had composed yourself, and you killed him. Unfortunately for you, in your haste to leave the place you dropped the letter in the street outside. I have it here."

Pulling the letter from his pocket, he held it out to de Menilmont. The comte looked at it with the aloof indifference of a medieval baron to whom a vassal was proffering an unworthy gift, but it seemed to Gautier that for the first time a tiny crack appeared in his composure. When he spoke his speech was quicker, his voice at a perceptibly higher pitch. "It is an ingenious theory you have constructed, Inspector, but you forget one thing."

"What is that?" Courtrand asked quickly, anxious no doubt to hear the comte exonerate himself.

"I had no possible reason for wishing to discredit Pontana, for wishing to destroy him as you suggest. He was a man who, perhaps unwisely I realize now, I befriended when he came to France."

"You had a very good reason," Gautier replied. "The most common of all motives for criminal offences, material gain. Pontana was getting in the way of your marriage to Mademoiselle de Saules, a marriage you desperately needed to save you from bankruptcy."

"But I did not know of the liaison between

Pontana and the lady," de Menilmont said, like a man laying down a card which he knows cannot be beaten. He turned towards Madame de Saules. "That is true, Renée, is it not?"

Gautier sensed that Madame de Saules was going to confirm what the comte had said. Loyalty to an old friend or the tribal instinct of the rich to protect themselves from the Philistines was strong enough to make her lie. He said quickly: "Before you answer, Madame, you should know that among the abbé's possessions we found the note which you wrote urging him to hasten his enquiries in Italy. In it you said how patient and understanding the comte was being about your daughter's behaviour with Pontana."

"I never mentioned the comte's name," she blurted out unthinkingly.

"No. You were being careful in your secret dealings with the abbé. You referred to "A". Now who else could that be? Not your husband because we know he was totally unaware of your daughter's affair. No, "A" stood for Albi, a family name of the comte's and one no doubt which his intimate friends sometimes used."

Embarrassed and appalled, Courtrand had played no part in a scene which must have seemed to him like a nightmare. Now he decided to intervene, hoping perhaps that the whole unpleasant business might turn out to be a misunderstanding and one that could be tidied away. He asked Gautier: "Can you prove this outrageous accusation?"

"There should be no difficulty in doing so, Monsieur le Directeur. The comte could not risk being seen leaving his home disguised as a woman, so he had the ingenious idea of going to a hotel in Rue St. Denis, the Hotel Cavour, a shady establishment used by pederasts of both sexes, transvestites and perverts. No one there would be surprised if a client arrived as a man and went out dressed as a woman. The comte may well have used the hotel on previous occasions for other purposes and he probably spent the night there before going out early in the morning to the church of Sainte Clothilde. We have traced the driver of the fiacre which took him there again last evening from Pontana's apartment."

"Mother of God!" Monsieur de Saules exclaimed. To a man of good, conservative, bourgeois upbringing the notion that a gentleman might know of and frequent hotels like the Hotel Cavour must have come as a disturbing shock.

"You may be thinking," Gautier told the comte, "that the management of the hotel will never admit you were there. Places like that have to be discreet and protect their clients. But there are ways to break their silence. A threat to close the hotel down is a great persuader. We also have the reward money which Monsieur de Saules kindly placed at our disposal. Your offer still stands, Monsieur, I take it."

"If you need the money, yes."

"The people who patronize the Hotel Cavour would sell their mothers for twenty thousand francs."

As he was nearing the end of what he had to say, Gautier could sense a subtle change in the mood of Monsieur and Madame de Saules and Courtrand. Up till then they had been listening to him with an incredulous fascination, like an audience watching a play with an extravagantly improbable but absorbing plot. Then as he described the comte's cold-blooded subterfuge, the sordid details of the hotel and homosexuals and transvestites, fantasy was turning into sickening reality.

The Comte de Menilmont seemed about to

speak but then changed his mind. Instead he looked towards Madame de Saules, the appealing look of a man desperate for support, hoping that she at least would stand by him. But at that precise moment she looked away. Gautier was certain that she did so only to conceal the emotion in her face, perhaps even to hide her tears at what her pride saw as another humiliation for her. But the comte misconstrued her gesture as aimed at him, a gesture of disgust and rejection. His arrogance and self-assurance disintegrated and his whole face seemed to sag, becoming the face of a man without hope.

"Very well," he said in a low voice. "I admit it. I killed the abbé and Ponzi as well."

"What are you saying?" Courtrand exclaimed.

"I am not ashamed of what I did." Slowly the comte gathered the threadbare remnants of defiance around him. "Why should I be? It was my duty, an obligation, to protect Mademoiselle de Saules."

"You could have done it like a gentleman," Monsieur de Saules said reproachfully. "You could have challenged him to a duel and killed him."

"No doubt. And would your daughter ever have spoken to me again?"

The banker had no answer. De Menilmont looked at him and said: "You need not concern yourself about me, Monsieur. I will not be the first of my family to face the guillotine. Two of my ancestors were executed during the Revolution. And I at least will have a trial conducted by the due processes of law." His mood seemed to change and some of his pride returned at the thought of his trial. It was as though he could already see himself behind the prisoner's bar in the great Assize Court in the Palais de Justice, facing the judges in their scarlet robes, contemptuous of the crowds who had come to watch.

"I will not defend myself against the charge," he went on. "I will not deign to. But I will make a speech that will go down in history; a speech that will make the self-important judges and the mealy-mouthed bourgeois lawyers be ashamed of their effrontery in daring to put me, a member of the oldest and noblest family in France, on trial."

Courtrand's expression hardened as he listened. Sneers at the legal profession and therefore, by extension, at the officers of the law were not to be endured, even from an aristocrat. He said to Monsieur de Saules: "Would it be possible for Gautier to use your telephone, Monsieur? I wish to have a police wagon brought here."

"By all means use my telephone, but is that really necessary? Could you not take the comte with you in your carriage? You might spare him the humiliation of a police wagon."

"No, Monsieur," the Comte de Menilmont said firmly. "Let them treat me like a common criminal. If my ancestors could ride to the guillotine in a tumbril, why should I not ride to prison in a police wagon?"

19

NOT long after mid-day Juliette and Gautier were sharing a bottle of wine in the Café St. Michel in the boulevard of that name. When he had collected her at her home, Gautier had intended to take Juliette to the Café Corneille, but on a sudden, cowardly impulse, he had changed his mind. She had come out without a hat and, absurd though he knew it was as a reason, it was this that had provoked his decision. He had been ready to face the banter of his friends for escorting a woman to the Corneille—women did not go to cafés—but for a respectable young woman to appear in public during the day while not wearing a hat was unthinkable.

The Café St. Michel was not unknown to him, for he had been there from time to time and was acquainted with a few of its regular customers. Luck was on his side and two or three of them nodded to him and took off their hats to Juliette when they arrived. No one would ever describe it as a lively café and today as usual the businessmen who frequented it were talking solemnly about the price of coal and wood and ostrich feathers.

"I am disappointed," Juliette said as she looked around them.

"For what reason?"

"Men are always telling me that today the art of conversation flourishes only in cafés, that in a café the conversation is far more brilliant, more sincere and more profound than in any literary salon. Well," she nodded towards the people who were sitting around them, "where is the oratory, the wit and the passionate argument?"

"Saturday is always a bad day in a café," Gautier replied lamely. "Many of the regular customers stay away on Saturdays."

"Then I shall have plenty of time to enjoy your company," Juliette said and smiled. "Unless of course you are in a hurry to return to duty."

"No. I am free for the rest of the day."

"Does that mean the Didier affair is closed?"

"Yes. The Comte de Menilmont has admitted killing both the abbé and Pontana's secretary."

"There has been another murder? When did this happen?"

"Last evening. And Pontana was arrested at

the Gare de Lyon by my chief. Then Marie-Thérèse de Saules climbed on to the top of one of the towers of Notre Dame intending to jump to her death. It was quite a night, I can tell you."

"Why didn't you tell me all this when you found me waiting at your apartment?"

Gautier smiled as he replied: "To be perfectly frank, I had other things on my mind."

She smiled too at the innuendo in his words. "Well, tell me now then."

He gave her a brief, factual account of the events of the previous night and of his confrontation with the Comte de Menilmont in the home of Monsieur de Saules that morning. Finally he told her that Daniele Pontana had been released by the Sûreté an hour previously, had collected his valises and made immediately for the railway station, leaving it to the authorities to bury Ponzi.

"He is in such a hurry to get away that he will not even stay for the funeral," Gautier concluded.

"If he is going back to Italy, someone must be paying his debts," Juliette observed. "It cannot be a publisher because his work does not command great sales and he is too unreliable for anyone to make him a substantial advance. It can only be a woman who is financing him."

"Yes." Gautier agreed and was thankful that she did not ask him the name of the woman.

"And what about the Comte de Menilmont?" Juliette asked. She did not seem particularly surprised that the comte should have killed two men. "How is he facing up to the disgrace of prison and arrest and trial?"

"In a curious way, he seemed almost glad."

"Glad? How could he be?"

"I suspect he prefers the shame of the guillotine to the shame of bankruptcy. Perhaps he does not even see it as a disgrace. All his life he has lived in the shadow of his ancestors."

"Oh, those precious ancestors."

"Life has never given him the chance to live up to them and it never would; no chance of military greatness or feudal power. No, I think he is beginning to see the notoriety of the guillotine as a kind of glory. He will die bravely, I'm sure of that."

Juliette shuddered, as though even then she were watching the scene when the comte would be taken from his prison cell at La Roquette and led, with his hands tied behind his back, to the naked blade suspended in the early morning air. Then she shrugged her shoulders and said: "I suppose I should be glad he has confessed. At least now I can no longer be suspected of killing the abbé." Gautier smiled but said nothing and she went on: "At one time you did suspect me, did you not?"

"Suspect? Suspicion? I am not sure I really know what the words mean. There were a number of people besides yourself who might conceivably have had a reason for killing Abbé Didier: Pontana, the comte, Marie-Thérèse de Saules, Madame Trocville, the Duchesse de Paiva. I never reached a point of thinking that it might be any one of them rather than the rest."

"But you must have supposed it was a woman rather than a man."

"Why?"

"Had you not been told that a mysterious woman in a veil had been seen leaving the church soon after the abbé was killed?"

"Yes, but I never discounted the possibility that it might have been a man in disguise. A veil is a very effective way of concealing a man's features and why should this person, although apparently young and vigorous, walk around hunched and bent, unless of course it was a man trying to appear much shorter in stature than he really was."

"Can the comte really have supposed that Pontana would be arrested, tried and guillotined for killing the abbé?"

"Probably not. I imagine he would have been satisfied if the Italian had been disgraced. If Pontana had been arrested, can you imagine what the newspapers would have made of it? Everything about him, his past, the suspicious death of his wife would have been unearthed and turned into headlines. No rational man would have ever believed that Pontana would be convicted and sentenced to death on the slender evidence of a violent quarrel, a skill with weapons and a flair for female impersonation."

"Is any man who sets out to kill ever wholly rational?"

"I suppose not. The comte's behaviour certainly was not. But one should remember what Pontana had done to him. Because of Pontana, the comte had not only lost his chance of marrying a fortune, a fortune he desperately needed, but he had suffered what must have been to a proud aristocrat the supreme humiliation of being rejected by a girl of bourgeois upbringing. He had been made to look ridiculous."

"Many people remarked at the time that he took the rebuff very well," Juliette said.

"Yes, he concealed his feelings well, perhaps too well."

"What do you mean?"

"He had been taught in his upbringing to restrain his emotions, to remain reserved and aloof. But what was happening behind that façade? Can't you imagine the turmoil of his feelings, his rage and hatred towards Pontana? They must have festered inside him and poisoned his reason."

"Till he had to try to destroy Pontana?"

"Yes. In similar circumstances many men might have tried to contrive a way of killing a rival or of having him killed by a hired assassin, but de Menilmont was not satisfied with anything so straightforward. He had to devise a plot, a medieval plot which hinged around the stabbing of a priest, the kind of plot which villainous nobles of the fourteenth century might have conceived. By then he was a little mad. He became obsessed with his plot. It had to succeed."

"So when it seemed as though Ponzi might frustrate it, Ponzi had to be killed as well?"

"Exactly."

Juliette leant back in her chair. She seemed much more at ease and more contented than he had ever seen her before and Gautier found himself wondering whether this could be because she was now also more mature, more of a complete woman. He put the idea from his mind as absurd. It was just vanity and he laughed at himself for imagining, even briefly, that he had the power to give a woman fulfilment in a single night.

"You must be very pleased with yourself," she commented suddenly and he was afraid for a moment that she had guessed what he was thinking, but she continued: "for deducing that it was the comte who had killed the abbé and Ponzi and for persuading—I almost said tricking—him into confessing."

Gautier shrugged his shoulders. "Crimes are very seldom solved by brilliant deduction, but by patience and good fortune. On this occasion we had more than our share of luck."

He knew that what he was saying was true. Even before the abbé was killed, chance had intervened when Madame Trocville and the

Duchesse de Paiva had worn identical dresses to the party at the Tir aux Pigeons. But for that, Sapin would not have tried to steal the duchesse's necklace and Gautier would not have discovered that the real jewels had been sold nor guessed the part she was playing in the affair between Pontana and Marie-Thérèse de Saules. It had been fortunate for Gautier also that Abbé Didier had left the note from Madame de Saules in the copy of Juliette's novel, for this had enabled him to make Madame de Saules admit that de Menilmont had known about the affair between her daughter and Pontana. Finally luck had come to his aid when the comte had dropped his fake letter in the street outside Pontana's apartment.

"I cannot help reminding myself," Gautier added, "that perhaps if I had used my powers of deduction sooner, Ponzi's death might have been avoided."

"I know you're not a vain man," Juliette replied, "but to carry self-criticism to those lengths is ridiculous."

Gautier smiled at the compliment. "I don't deserve the high opinion you seem to hold of me," he said lightly, "but I hope it won't change as we get to know each other better."

Juliette's expression changed. She had been smiling and he thought he could read much in her smile; contentment at the memory of the pleasure they had shared, expectancy of pleasure to come, even affection. Now the smile vanished and was replaced by a look which he had often seen on the faces of other people but never on hers, a look that was a compound of guiltiness and gloom.

She said abruptly: "You won't count on me too much, will you?"

"In what way?"

"Don't count on getting to know me."

"Is that a sophisticated way of ending an affair?" he asked without bitterness.

"Of course it isn't! How ridiculous! You're being stupid!" she said. Then her little spurt of anger subsided and she touched his hand gently. "I'm trying to warn you, that's all."

"About what?"

"I want you, Jean-Paul, but I want you selfishly because you see I can never give myself completely to anyone."

"I can't believe that."

"Not very long ago my father died. He was the person I loved more than anything else in life. I went home and sat beside his bed and watched him die. Can you imagine my grief? And yet all the time part of me remained detached, observing him as he died, observing my own grief, recording it in my memory." Juliette shook her head as though even now she could not believe or understand her heartlessness. "And one day, no doubt, when the grief is no longer real, it will all appear thinly disguised in a book."

Gautier understood what she was trying to say. "Was it like that last night?" he asked bluntly.

"Yes."

Picking up the carafe of wine which stood on the table between them, he filled their glasses. Juliette said: "You deserve better than that. I'm sorry."

She was being honest and he contrasted her honesty with his own petty dishonesty, his deception in bringing her to the Café St. Michel instead of taking her to the Corneille, for fear of the ridicule of his friends. Moreover what she had said about herself was also true of him. An inner constraint had always forced him to conceal part of his thoughts and emotions from other people, to hold back from true intimacy.

That was the real reason, he knew now, why his marriage had failed.

"I understand. And I won't ask too much of you," he told Juliette, and as he spoke he felt the shadow of loneliness at his back.

THE END

Other titles in the
Linford Mystery Library:

STORM CENTRE
by Douglas Clark

Detective Chief Superintendent Masters, temporarily lecturing in a police staff college, finds there's more to the job than a few weeks' relaxation in a rural setting. He soon gets involved in a local police problem.

THE MANUSCRIPT MURDERS
by Roy Harley Lewis

Antiquarian bookseller Matthew Coll, acquires a rare 16th century manuscript. But when the Dutch professor who had discovered the journal is murdered, Coll begins to doubt its authenticity.

SHARENDEL
by Margaret Carr

Ruth had loved Aunt Cass. She didn't want all that money. And she didn't want Aunt Cass to die. But at Sharendel things looked different. She began to wonder if she had a split personality.

MURDER TO BURN
by Laurie Mantell

Sergeants Steven Arrow and Lance Brendon, of the New Zealand police force, come upon a woman's body floating in the water. When the dead woman is finally identified the police begin to realise that they are investigating a fascinatingly complex fraud.

YOU CAN HELP ME
by Maisie Birmingham

Whilst running the Citizens' Advice Bureau, Kate Weatherley is attacked with no apparent motive. Then the body of one of her clients is found in her room.

DAGGERS DRAWN
by Margaret Carr

Stacey Manston was the kind of girl who could take most things in her stride, but three murders were something different — especially as she had the motive and opportunity to kill them all . . .

THE MONTMARTRE MURDERS
by Richard Grayson

Inspector Gautier of Sûreté investigates the disappearance of artist Théo, the heir to a fortune. Then a shady art dealer is murdered and the plot begins to focus on three paintings by a seemingly obscure artist.

GRIZZLY TRAIL
by Gwen Moffat

Miss Pink, alone in the Rockies, helps in a search for missing hikers, solves two cruel murders and has the most terrifying experience of her life when she meets a grizzly bear!

BLINDMAN'S BLUFF
by Margaret Carr

Kate Deverill had considered suicide. It was one way out—and preferable to being murdered. Better than waiting for the blow to strike, waiting and wondering . . .

BEGOTTEN MURDER
by Martin Carroll

When Susan Phillips joined her aunt on a voyage of 12,000 miles from her home in Melbourne, she little knew their arrival would germinate the seeds of murder planted long ago.